Paddington Children's Hospital

Caring for children—and captivating hearts!

The doctors and nurses of
Paddington Children's Hospital are renowned
for their expert care of their young patients,
no matter the cost. And now, as they face
both a heart-wrenching emergency
and a dramatic fight to save their hospital,
the stakes are higher than ever!

Devoted to their jobs, these talented
professionals are about to discover that saving
lives can often mean risking your heart…

Available now in the thrilling
Paddington Children's Hospital miniseries:

Their One Night Baby
by Carol Marinelli

Forbidden to the Playboy Surgeon
by Fiona Lowe

Mummy, Nurse…Duchess?
by Kate Hardy

Falling for the Foster Mum
by Karin Baine

And coming soon…

Healing the Sheikh's Heart
by Annie O'Neil

A Life-Saving Reunion
by Alison Roberts

Dear Reader,

I was thrilled when my editor asked me to be part of the Paddington Children's Hospital series. I love working with other authors to build a world, and I was even happier to find that part of my book was going to be set in Italy—which is one of my favourite parts of the world.

It was also great fun to write about small children again—I loved reliving the days when mine enjoyed going to the park and the aquarium. And one of my best friends had twins a couple of months after I had my eldest, so that brought back memories too.

But Leo and Rosie have a lot of obstacles to overcome from their pasts before they can find happiness—and they're surprised to discover that being with each other is just the way to do it. So when Leo sweeps Rosie off to a glamorous ball he discovers that the castle where he grew up is much better filled with the laughter of children—and Rosie discovers that... Well, you'll have to read the book to find out!

I'm always delighted to hear from readers, so do come and visit me at katehardy.com or chat to me on Facebook.

With love,

Kate Hardy

MUMMY, NURSE... DUCHESS?

BY
KATE HARDY

First published in Great Britain 2017
By Mills & Boon, an imprint of HarperCollins*Publishers*
1 London Bridge Street, London, SE1 9GF

Large Print edition 2017

© 2017 Harlequin Books S.A.

Special thanks and acknowledgement are given to Kate Hardy for her contribution to the Paddington Children's Hospital series.

ISBN: 978-0-263-06731-6

MIX
Paper from
responsible sources
FSC™ C007454

Kate Hardy has always loved books, and could read before she went to school. She discovered Mills & Boon books when she was twelve and decided this was what she wanted to do. When she isn't writing Kate enjoys reading, cinema, ballroom dancing and the gym. You can contact her via her website: katehardy.com.

Books by Kate Hardy

Mills & Boon Medical Romance

Christmas Miracles in Maternity

The Midwife's Pregnancy Miracle

Her Playboy's Proposal
Capturing the Single Dad's Heart

Mills & Boon Cherish

Holiday with the Best Man
Falling for the Secret Millionaire
Her Festive Doorstep Baby

Visit the Author Profile page
at millsandboon.co.uk for more titles.

To my fellow PCH authors, who made
writing this such an enjoyable experience.

CHAPTER ONE

Paddington Children's Hospital

THE REDBRICK BUILDING loomed before Leo in the street; the turret, with its green dome, reminded him so much of Florence that it was almost enough to make him miss Tuscany. Then again, London had felt more like home than Florence, ever since he'd first come to study medicine here as a teenager.

As the car pulled to a halt, Leo could see Robyn Kelly waiting outside the hospital gates for him, her curly blonde hair gleaming brightly in the sun. When the Head of Surgery had asked him to come to Paddington to help out in the aftermath of the fire that had ripped through a local children's school, of course he'd said yes. Robyn had taken him under her wing when he'd been on his first rotation and had been feeling just a little bit lost; back then, he'd appreciated her kindness. And he'd also appreciated the fact that she'd seen him as a doctor first and a duke second, treating him as part of the team rather than as a special case.

This was his chance to pay just a little of that back.

There was a small group of protestors standing outside the gate, holding placards: 'Save Our Hospital' and 'Kids' Health Not Wealth'.

Which was one of the reasons why his contract was temporary: Paddington Children's Hospital was under threat of closure, with a plan to merge the staff and patients with Riverside Hospital. Not because the one-hundred-and-fifty-year-old hospital wasn't needed any more—the fact that the place was full to overflowing after the recent fire at Westbourne Grove Primary School proved just how much the hospital was needed—but because the Board of Governors had had a lucrative offer for the site. So, instead of keeping the hospital as an important part of the community, they planned to sell it so it could be turned into a block of posh apartments. The Board of Governors had already run staff numbers down in anticipation of the merger, to the point where everyone was struggling to cope.

Leo's lip curled. He'd grown up in a world where money didn't just talk, it shouted, and that disgusted him. It was the main reason why he was drawn to philanthropic medicine now: so he could give some of that privilege back. So when Robyn had explained the situation at Paddington's to him and said they needed someone with a high profile to come and work with them and get the hospital's plight into international news, Leo had had no hesitation in agreeing. It was a chance to use the heritage he loathed for a good cause.

Even though he knew the waiting photographers weren't there to take pictures of the protestors, Leo intended to make quite sure that the protestors and the placards were in every single shot. The more publicity for this cause, the better. So, right at this moment, he was here in his role as the Duke of Calvanera rather than being plain Dr Marchetti. And that was why he was meeting Robyn outside the hospital gates in the middle of the morning, instead of being two hours into his shift. This was all about getting maximum publicity.

He took a deep breath and opened the door of the sleek, black car.

'Your Highness!' one of the photographers called as Leo emerged from the car. 'Over here!'

Years of practice meant that it was easy enough for him to deflect the photographers with an awkward posture, until he reached Robyn and the protestors. Robyn had clearly primed the picket line, because they crowded behind him with their placards fully visible; there was no way that any photograph of his face wouldn't contain at least a word or two from a placard. And then he shook Robyn's hand, looked straight at the cameras and smiled as the bulbs flashed.

'Is it true you're coming to work here?' one of the journalists called.

'Yes,' he said.

'Why Paddington?' another called.

'Because it's important. The hospital has been here for a hundred and fifty years, looking after the children in the city. And it needs to stay here, instead of being merged with Riverside Hospital, outside the city,' he answered.

'Moving the patients to Riverside means the kids will have better facilities than at this old place,' one of the journalists pointed out.

'State of the art, you mean?' Leo asked. 'But when it comes to medicine, *time's* the most important thing. You can have the most cutting edge equipment in the world—but if your patient doesn't reach those facilities in time, all that fancy stuff isn't going to be able to save a life. It'll be too late.'

The journalist went red and shuffled his feet.

'You don't need flashy equipment and modern buildings to be a good hospital,' Leo said. 'You need to be *accessible*. What would've happened to the children of Westbourne Grove Primary School if Paddington had been closed? How many of them wouldn't have made it to those lovely new buildings and all the state-of-the-art equipment at Riverside in time to be treated?'

He was met with silence as the press clearly worked out the answer for themselves.

'Exactly. And I'm very happy for you all to quote me saying that,' he said softly. 'Talk to these guys.' He gestured to the protestors, knowing from Robyn that several of them had been treated here years ago and others had recently had their own children treated here. 'Find out their stories. They're much more interesting and much more important than I am.'

'I think you made your point,' Robyn said as they walked into the hospital together.

'Good,' Leo said as she led him in to the department where he was going to be working, ready to introduce him to everyone. 'Paddington's is an important facility. An outstanding facility. And I'll do everything I can to help you publicise that.'

Rosie Hobbes stifled a cynical snort as she overheard the Duke of Calvanera's comment. Who was he trying to kid? More like, he was trying to raise his own profile. Why would someone like him—a rich, powerful playboy—care about the fate of an old London hospital?

She knew he'd agreed to come and help at Paddington's because he'd trained with Robyn, years ago; but it was still pretty hard to believe that an actual duke would want to do a job like this. Who would want to work in a hospital that was currently full to the brim with patients but badly understaffed because the Board of Directors hadn't replaced anyone who'd left, in line with their plan to move everyone out and sell the place?

Especially a man who was so good-looking and seemed so charming.

Rosie knew all about how charm and good looks could hide a rotten heart. Been there, done that, and her three-year-old twins were the ones who'd nearly paid the price.

Thinking of the twins made her heart skip a beat, and she caught her breath. It had been just over a year now, and she still found panic coursing through her when she remembered that night. The threats. The dead look behind that man's eyes. The way he'd looked at her children as if they were merely a means to getting what he wanted instead of seeing them as the precious lives they were.

She dug her nails into her palms. Focus, Rosie, she told herself. Freddie and Lexi were absolutely fine. If there was any kind of problem with either of the twins, the hospital nursery school would've called her straight away. The place was completely secure; only the staff inside could open the door, and nobody could take a child without either being on the list as someone with permission to collect a child, or giving the emergency code word for any particular child. Michael was dead, so his associates couldn't threaten the twins—or Rosie—any more. And right now she had a job to do.

'Everything all right, Rosie?' Robyn asked.

'Sure,' Rosie said. Her past was *not* going to interfere with her new life here. She was a survivor, not a victim.

'I just wanted to introduce you to Leo,' Robyn continued. 'He'll be working with us for the next couple of months.'

Or until something even more high profile came along, Rosie thought. Maybe she was judging him unfairly but, in her experience, handsome playboys couldn't be trusted.

'Leo, this is Rosie Hobbes, one of our paediatric nurses. Rosie, this is Leo Marchetti,' Robyn said.

'Hello,' Rosie said, and gave him a cool nod.

He gave her the sexiest smile she'd ever seen, and his dark eyes glittered with interest. 'Delighted to meet you, *signora*,' he said.

Rosie would just bet he'd practised that smile

in front of the mirror. And he'd hammed up that Italian accent to make himself sound super-sexy; she was sure he hadn't had an accent at all when he'd walked onto the ward with Robyn. She should just think herself lucky he hadn't bowed and kissed her hand. Or was that going to be next?

'Welcome to Paddington's, Your Highness,' she said.

He gave her another of those super-charming smiles. 'Here, I'm a doctor, not a duke. "Leo" will do just fine.'

'Dr Marchetti,' she said firmly, hoping she'd made it clear that she preferred to keep her work relationships very professional indeed. 'Excuse me—I really need to review these charts following the ward round. Enjoy your first day at the Castle.'

The Castle? Was she making a pointed comment about where he came from? Leo wondered. But women weren't usually sharp with him. They usually smiled back, responding to his warmth. He liked women—a lot—and they liked him.

Why had Rosie Hobbes cut him dead? Had he done something to upset her?

But he definitely hadn't met her before. He would've remembered her—and not just because she was tall, curvy and pretty, with that striking copper hair in a tousled bob, and those vivid blue eyes. There was something challenging about Rosie. Something that made him want to get up close and personal with her and find out exactly what made her tick.

She hadn't been wearing a wedding ring. Not that that meant anything, nowadays. Was she single?

And why was he wondering that in any case? He was here to do a job. Relationships weren't on the agenda, especially with someone he worked with. He was supposed to be finding someone suited to his position: another European noble, or perhaps the heir to a business empire. And together they would continue the Marchetti dynasty by producing a son.

Right now, he still couldn't face that. He wasn't ready to trap someone else in the castle where he'd grown up, lonely and miserable and desperate for his father's approval—approval that his father had been quick to withhold if Leo did or said anything wrong. Though what was wrong one day was right on another. Leo had never been able to work out what his father actually wanted. All he'd known for sure was that he was a disappointment to the Duke.

He shook himself. Now wasn't the time to be thinking about that. 'Thank you,' he said, giving Rosie his warmest smile just for the hell of it, and followed Robyn to be introduced to the rest of the staff on the ward.

Once Rosie had finished reviewing the charts and typing notes into the computer, she headed on to the ward. Hopefully Dr Marchetti would be on the next ward by now, meeting and greeting, and she could just get on with her job.

Why had he rattled her so much? She wasn't one to be bowled over and breathless just because a man was good-looking. Not any more. Leo had classic movie-star looks: tall, with dark eyes and short, neat dark hair. He was also charming and confident, and Rosie had learned the hard way that charm couldn't be trusted. Her whirlwind marriage had turned into an emotional rollercoaster, and she'd promised herself never to make that mistake again. So, even if Leo Marchetti was good friends with their Head of Surgery, Rosie intended to keep him at a very professional distance.

She dropped into one of the bays to check on Penelope Craig. Penny was one of their long-term patients, and the little girl had been admitted to try and get her heart failure under control after an infection had caused her condition to worsen.

'How are you doing, Penny?' Rosie asked.

The little girl looked up from her drawing and gave her the sweetest, sweetest smile. 'Nurse Rosie! I'm fine, thank you.'

Rosie exchanged a glance with Julia, Penny's mother. They both knew it wasn't true, but Penny wasn't a whiner. She'd become a firm favourite on the ward, always drawing special pictures and chattering about kittens and ballet. 'That's good,' she said. 'I just need to do—'

'—my obs,' Penny finished. 'I know.'

Rosie checked Penny's pulse, temperature and oxygen sats. 'That's my girl. Oh, and I've got something for you.' She reached into her pocket and brought out a sheet of stickers.

'Kittens! I love kittens,' Penny said with a beaming smile. 'Thank you so much. Look, Mummy.'

'They're lovely,' Julia said, but Rosie could see the strain and weariness behind her smile. She understood only too well how it felt to worry about your children; being helpless to do any-thing to fix the problems must be sheer hell.

'Thank you, Rosie,' Julia added.

'Pleasure.' Rosie winked at Penny. 'Hopefully these new drugs will have you back on your feet soon.' The little girl was desperate to be a bal-lerina, and wore a pink tutu even when she was bed-bound. And Rosie really, really hoped that the little girl would have time for her dreams to come true. 'Call me if you need anything,' Rosie added to Julia.

'I will. Thanks.'

Rosie checked on the rest of the children in her bay, and was writing up the notes when her col-league Kathleen came over to the desk.

'So have you met the Duke, yet?' Kathleen fanned herself. 'Talk about film-star good looks.'

Rosie rolled her eyes. 'Handsome is as hand-some does.' And never again would she let a handsome, charming man treat her as a second-class citizen.

'Give the guy a break,' Kathleen said. 'He seems a real sweetie. And his picture is already all over the Internet, with the "Save Our Hospital" placards in full view. I think Robyn's right and he's really going to help.'

Rosie forced herself to smile. 'Good.'

Kathleen gave her a curious look. 'Are you all right, Rosie?'

'Sure. I had a bit of a broken night,' Rosie fibbed. 'Lexi had a bad dream and it was a while before I got back to sleep again.'

'I really don't know how you do it,' Kathleen said. 'It's tough enough, being a single mum—but having twins must make it twice as hard.'

'I get double the joy and double the love,' Rosie said. 'I wouldn't miss a single minute. And my parents and my sister are great—I know I can call on them if I get stuck.'

'Even so. You must miss your husband so much.'

Rosie had found that it was much easier to let people think that she was a grieving widow than to tell them the truth—that she'd been planning to divorce Michael Duncan before his death, and after his death she'd reverted back to her maiden name, changing the children's names along with hers. 'Yes,' Rosie agreed. And it wasn't a total lie. She missed the man she'd thought she'd married—not the one behind the mask, the one who put money before his babies and his wife.

She was busy on the ward for the rest of the morning and didn't see Leo again until lunchtime.

'I believe we'll be working closely together,' the Duke said.

She rather hoped he was wrong.

'So I thought maybe we could have lunch together and get to know each other a bit better,' he added.

'Sorry,' Rosie said. 'I'm afraid I have a previous engagement.' Just as she did every Monday, Wednesday and Friday when Penny was in the hospital.

He looked as if he hoped she'd be polite and invite him to join her in whatever she was doing. Well, tough. This wasn't about him. It was about her patient. 'I'm sure Kathleen or one of the others would be very happy for you to join them in the canteen,' she said.

'Thank you. Then I'll go and find them,' he said, with that same charming smile.

And Rosie felt thoroughly in the wrong.

But Leo had already turned away and it was too late to call him back and explain.

Why was Rosie Hobbes so prickly with him? Leo wondered. Everyone else at Paddington Children's Hospital had seemed pleased that he'd joined the team and had welcomed him warmly. Everyone except Rosie.

Did she hate all men?

Possibly not, because earlier he'd seen her talking to Thomas Wolfe, the cardiology specialist, and she'd seemed perfectly relaxed.

And why was he so bothered when she was just one member of the team? Wherever you worked, there was always a spectrum: people you got on really well with, people you liked and people you had to grit your teeth and put up with. He was obviously one of the latter, where Rosie was concerned, even though today was the first time they'd met. He knew he ought to just treat her with the calm professionalism he reserved for people who rubbed him up the wrong way. But he couldn't help asking about her when he was sitting in the canteen with a couple of the junior doctors and two of the nurses.

'So Rosie doesn't usually join you?' he asked.

'Not when Penny's in,' Kathleen said.

'Penny?'

'You must've seen her when Robyn took you round,' Kathleen said. 'One of our patients. Six years old, brown hair in plaits and the most amazing eyes—grey, with this really distinctive rim?'

Leo shook his head. 'Sorry. It doesn't ring a bell.'

'Well, you'll definitely get to know her while you're here. She has heart failure, and she's been in and out of here for months,' Kathleen explained. 'She's a total sweetheart. Rosie's one of the nurses who always looks after her. When she's in on a Monday, Wednesday or Friday, Rosie spends her lunch break reading her ballet stories.'

'Because the little girl likes ballet, I presume?' Leo asked.

'Lives and breathes it. And also it gives her

mum or dad a break, depending on who's taken the time off to be with her,' Kathleen explained.

'So Penny's special to Rosie?'

'She's special to all of us,' Kathleen said. 'If you've seen any drawings pinned up in the staff room or the office, nine times out of ten it'll be one of Penny's.'

'Right.' Leo wondered why Rosie hadn't told him that herself. Or maybe she'd thought he'd have a go at her for being unprofessional and showing too much favouritism to a patient.

He chatted easily with the others until the end of their lunch break, then headed back to the ward. The first person he saw was Rosie, who he guessed had just left her little patient.

'So did Penny enjoy her story?' he asked.

Colour flooded into her cheeks. 'How do you know about that?'

'Kathleen said you have a regular lunch date with her when you're in.'

'It gives Julia and Peter—her parents—a chance to get out of here for a few minutes to get some fresh air,' she said. 'And it isn't a problem with Robyn.'

So she *had* thought he'd disapprove of the way

she spent her lunch break. 'It's very kind of you,' he said. Was it just because Penny was a favourite with the staff, or did Rosie maybe have a sister who'd gone through something similar? It was too intrusive to ask. He needed to tread carefully with Rosie or she'd back away from him again.

'She's a lovely girl.'

'Maybe you can tell me about her after work,' he said. 'I hear there's a nice pub across the road. The Frog and...?' He paused, not remembering the name.

'Peach,' she supplied. 'Sorry. I can't.'

Can't or won't? he wondered. 'Another previous engagement?'

'Actually, yes.'

Another patient? He didn't think she'd tell him. 'That's a shame. Some other time.'

But she didn't suggest a different day or time.

He really ought to just give up.

A couple of his new colleagues had already made it clear that they'd be happy to keep him company if he was lonely. It could be fun to take them up on their offers, as long as they understood that he didn't do permanent relationships.

Except there was something about Rosie

Hobbes that drew him. It wasn't just that she was one of the few women who didn't respond to him; his ego could stand the odd rejection. But she intrigued him, and he couldn't work out why. Was it that she was so different from the women he was used to, women who swooned over him or flattered him because he was a duke? Or was it something deeper?

It had been a long time since someone had intrigued him like this. Something more than just brief sexual attraction. And that in himself made him want to explore it further—to understand what made Rosie tick, and also why he felt this weird pull towards her.

Tomorrow, he thought. He'd try talking to her again tomorrow.

Rosie was five minutes late from her shift, and the twins were already waiting for her with their backpacks on. They were singing something with Nina, one of the nursery school assistants, who was clearly teaching them actions to go with the song. Rosie felt a rush of love for them. Her twins were so different: Lexi, bouncy and confident, with a mop of blonde curls that reminded Rosie a little too much of Michael, and yet other than that she was the double of Rosie at that age. And Freddie, quieter and a little shy, with the same curls as his sister except mid-brown instead of golden, and her own bright blue eyes; thankfully he hadn't turned out to be Michael's double. Rosie was determined that her children were going to know nothing but love and happiness for the rest of their lives—and she really hoped that they wouldn't remember what life had been like when their father was around.

'Mummy!' The second they saw her, Lexi and Freddie rushed over to her and flung their arms round her.

'My lovely Lexi and Freddie.' Rosie felt as if she could breathe properly again, now she was back with her babies. Even though she loved her job and she knew the twins were well looked after in the nursery school attached to the hospital, she was much happier with them than she was away from them.

'So what have you been doing today?' she asked, holding one hand each as they walked out of the hospital.

'We singed.' Lexi demonstrated the first verse

of 'The Wheels on the Bus,' completely out of tune and at full volume.

'That's lovely, darling,' Rosie said.

'And we had Play-Doh,' Freddie added. 'I maked a doggie. A plurple one.'

Rosie hid a smile at his adorable mispronunciation. 'Beautiful,' she said. She knew how badly her son wanted a dog of their own, but it just wasn't possible with their current lifestyle. It wouldn't be fair to leave a dog alone all day; and she couldn't leave the twins alone while she took the dog for the kind of long walk it would need after being cooped up all day, and which the twins would be too tired to do after a day at nursery school.

'We had cookies,' Lexie said.

'Chocolate ones. Nina maked them. They were crum—crum—' Freddie added, frowning when he couldn't quite remember the new word.

Crumbly? Or maybe a longer word. 'Nina made them,' Rosie corrected gently, 'and they were scrumptious, yes?' she guessed.

'Crumshus!' Lexie crowed. 'That's right.'

The twins chattered all the way on the short Tube journey and then the ten-minute walk home.

They were still chattering when Rosie cooked their tea, and gave them a bath. Although Freddie was a little on the shy side with strangers, he strove to match his more confident sister at home.

And Rosie was happy to let them chatter and laugh. She'd worried every day for the last year that their experience with Michael's associate had scarred them; but hopefully they'd been too young to realise quite what was going on and how terrified their mother had been.

Once the twins were in bed, she curled up on the sofa with a cup of tea and a puzzle magazine. A year ago, she would never have believed she could be this relaxed again. Some things hadn't changed; she was still the one who did everything for the twins and did all the cooking and cleaning. But she no longer had to deal with Michael's mercurial mood swings, his scorn and his contempt, and that made all the difference. Being a single parent was hard, but she had the best family and good friends to support her. And she didn't have Michael to undermine her confidence all the time.

Various friends had hinted that she ought to start dating again. Part of Rosie missed the closeness of having a partner, someone to cuddle into at stupid o'clock in the morning when she woke from a bad dream. But she'd lost her trust in relationships. Good ones existed, she knew; she'd seen it with her parents and with friends. But Rosie herself had got it so badly wrong with Michael that she didn't trust her judgement any more. Trusting another man, after the mess of her marriage, would be hard. Too hard. Plus, she had the twins to consider. So she'd become good at turning the conversation to a different subject rather than disappointing her well-meaning friends and family, and any direct suggestions of a date were firmly met with 'Sorry, no.'

Just as she'd rebuffed Leo Marchetti this evening, when he'd suggested that they went for a drink in the pub over the road after work.

Had she been too hard on him?

OK, so the guy was a charmer, something that set all her inner alarm bells clanging. On the other hand, today had been Leo's first day at Paddington's. The only person he knew at the hospital was Robyn, so he was probably feeling a bit lost. Guilt nagged at her. She'd been pretty abrupt with him, and it wasn't his fault he'd been born with a Y chromosome and was full of charm. She needed to lighten up. Maybe she'd suggest having lunch with him tomorrow.

But she'd make it clear that lunch meant lunch only. She wasn't in a position to offer anything more. And, if she was honest with herself, it'd be a long time before she was ready to trust anyone with anything more. If ever.

CHAPTER TWO

'YOU'RE IN CLINIC with Rosie, this morning,' Kathleen said to Leo with a smile when he walked onto the ward. 'It's the allergy and immunology clinic.'

'Great. Just point me in the right direction,' he said, smiling back.

Hopefully Rosie would be less prickly with him today. And if they could establish a decent working relationship, then he might be able to work out why she drew him so much, and he could deal with it the way he always dealt with things. With a charming smile and a little extra distance.

He looked through the files while he waited for Rosie to turn up.

'Sorry, sorry,' she said, rushing in. 'I was held up this morning.'

'You're not late,' he pointed out, though he was

pleased that she didn't seem quite so defensive with him today.

'No, but...' She flapped a dismissive hand. 'Has anyone told you about today's clinic?'

'Kathleen said it was the allergy and immunology clinic, so I'm assuming some of these patients have been coming here for a while.'

'They have,' she confirmed.

'Then at least they have some continuity with you,' he said with a smile. 'Are you happy to call our first patient in?'

Their first patient was an eighteen-month-old girl, Gemma Chandler. 'The doctor asked me last time to keep a food diary with a symptom chart,' her mother said.

'May I see them, please?' Leo asked.

She took it out of her bag and handed it to him; he read the document carefully. 'So she tends to get tummy pain, wind and diarrhoea, and sometimes her tummy feels bloated to you.'

Mrs Chandler nodded. 'And sometimes she's come out in a rash on her face and it's been itchy. It's really hard to stop her scratching it.'

'There are some lotions that help with the itch and last a bit longer than calamine lotion,' Leo said. 'I can write you a prescription for that. And you've done a really good job on the diary—I can see a very clear link between what she's eating and her symptoms.'

'It's dairy, isn't it?' Mrs Chandler bit her lip. 'I looked it up on the Internet.'

'The Internet's useful,' Leo said, 'but there are also a lot of scare stories out there and a lot of wrong information, so I'm glad you came to see us as well. Yes, I think it's an allergy to dairy— more specifically lactose intolerance. What that means is that Gemma's body doesn't have enough of the enzyme lactase to deal with any lactose in the body—that's the sugar in milk. What I think we need to do is try an exclusion diet for the next fortnight to confirm it. So that means I'd like you to check the labels for everything and make sure there's no milk in anything she eats or drinks. If you can keep doing the food diary and symptom chart, we can review everything in a fortnight.'

'We can give you some information leaflets about substitutes and vitamin supplements,' Rosie said. 'You can give Gemma rice milk instead of cow's milk, and sunflower margarine instead of butter.'

'Gemma's meant to be going to her cousin's birthday party, next week.' Mrs Chandler sighed. 'So that's going to be difficult—she won't be able to have any of the sandwiches or any of the cake, will she?'

'You could do a special packed lunch for her,' Rosie suggested. 'And I'm sure if you tell your family and friends, they'll help you work things out.' She handed Mrs Chandler a leaflet. 'Eating out with a toddler can be tricky enough, but having to take a food allergy into account can make it seem overwhelming.'

Was she talking from personal experience? Leo wondered. Or was it because she'd worked with so many patients in the allergy clinic? Not that he could ask without being intrusive, and he didn't want to give Rosie any excuse to back away from him.

'There are some good websites on the back of the leaflet for helping you to find places where they offer dairy-free options,' Rosie said.

'Thank you,' Mrs Chandler said.

'And we'll see you and Gemma again in a fortnight to see how things are. If her symptoms are better,' Leo said, 'I'll refer you to a dietitian so you can get proper support with a long-term exclusion diet. And in the meantime, if you have any questions or you're worried about anything, give us a call.'

Mrs Chandler nodded. 'Will she ever grow out of it? I've heard that some children do.'

'We really can't tell, right now,' Leo admitted. 'I think this is something we'll need to take one step at a time.'

Once the Chandlers had gone, while Leo was writing up the case notes, Rosie got out the next patient's notes. 'Sammy Kennedy. He's a sweetheart.'

'What's he seeing us about?' Leo asked.

'He has CAPS.'

Cryopyrin-Associate Periodic Syndrome. Leo knew it was an auto-inflammation disorder where the immune system was overactive and caused prolonged periods of inflammation, rather than the body producing antibodies against itself. 'That's rare,' he said. 'About one in a million. Actually, I've only seen one case before.'

'Sammy's my only case, too,' she said. 'Most patients with CAPS in the UK have Muckle-Wells Syndrome, and that's the variant Sammy has.'

'Tell me about him,' Leo invited. Sure, he could read the file, but this way he got the chance to interact with Rosie. And he liked how quick her mind was.

'He's eight years old and he's been coming here for nearly a year. He comes to clinic with his mum roughly every eight weeks. We check his knees and ankles and do bloods to measure the inflammation levels, and then we give him an injection of the drug that keeps his MWS under control,' she explained.

'That's the drug that blocks interleukin 1β, yes?' he checked.

'Yes,' she confirmed. 'The treatment's still new enough that we don't know the long-term effects, but we're hoping that it will stop more severe problems developing as he grows older.'

'Such as deafness?'

'Exactly,' she said. 'Are you ready to see him now?'

He nodded. 'Absolutely.'

Rosie went out into the reception area and came back with Sammy and his mother.

Leo smiled at them. 'Hello. I'm Dr Marchetti—

you can call me Dr Leo, if you prefer. And you're Sammy?'

The little boy nodded.

'Tell me how you're doing, Sammy,' Leo invited.

'Sometimes I have good days, and sometimes I get bad days,' Sammy said, shrugging.

'OK. What happens when you have a bad day?'

'Mum says it's a flare-up. It affects my tummy, my knees and my head. I get a rash, and it's always at night.' Sammy grimaced. 'Show him, Mum.'

Mrs Kennedy took out her phone and showed them a picture of the nettle rash on Sammy's stomach.

'How often do you get flare-ups?' Leo asked.

'Every couple of weeks. But it's not been so bad, lately.'

'Are you happy for us to examine you?' Leo asked.

Sammy gave him a rueful smile. 'I know the drill. You ask me questions, look me over, take blood and then give me the injections.'

'That's a pretty good summary,' Leo said, smiling back.

'I don't like the injections,' Sammy said. 'They sting and they make my skin sore. But I guess it's better than the rash.'

'A lot of people don't like injections, so you're not alone there,' Leo said. 'Is there anything you'd like to add or ask, Mrs Kennedy?'

'We're getting to be old hands at this, now,' she said. 'It's fine.'

Between them, Rosie and Leo examined Sammy, and she took a blood sample. Then Leo administered the drug.

Sammy flinched.

'I'm sorry it stings,' Leo said.

'It's all right,' Sammy said, clearly trying to be brave.

'I have something for you,' Rosie said. 'That is… Unless you're too old to have a lolly for being brave?'

Sammy grinned when he saw the red and white lolly. 'As if I'm going to turn down a lolly. Especially when it's in my team's colours!'

'You're a football fan?' Leo asked.

Sammy nodded. 'I'd like to be a footballer, but my CAPS is going to get in the way a bit, and I don't want to let my team down. But I guess I could be a scientist when I grow up and invent a needle that doesn't hurt when you give someone an injection.'

'That,' Leo said, 'is a brilliant idea, and I think it deserves something extra.' He produced another red and white lolly. 'Don't tell Rosie I raided her lolly jar,' he said in a stage whisper.

Sammy laughed. 'See you in a couple of months, Dr Leo.'

'See you,' Leo returned with a smile.

When the Kennedys had left, he looked at Rosie. 'Sammy's a nice kid.'

'He is,' she agreed. Then she paused. 'I was a bit abrupt with you yesterday. Sorry. So, um, I was wondering, would you like to have lunch with me today? Just as colleagues,' she added hastily.

Again he glanced at her left hand and saw no sign of a wedding ring. Did she really mean having lunch together just as colleagues, or did she feel the same pull of attraction towards him that he felt towards her?

It might explain why she'd been so prickly yesterday; she might be just as spooked by her reaction to him as he was by his reaction to her.

Though quite where they went from here, he had no idea. What he'd seen of Rosie so far told him that she was very professional—straight-talking, yet deeply caring towards her patients. He liked that. A lot.

But he also had the strongest impression that Rosie Hobbes wasn't the sort to have a casual fling. Which meant she was off limits, because he wasn't looking for something serious and long-term.

'Just as colleagues,' he agreed.

Once they'd seen the last patient at the clinic, they headed for the canteen. Leo noted that she chose a healthy salad and a mug of green tea—not that his own sandwich and coffee were *that* unhealthy. But Rosie clearly looked after her health.

'So how are you settling in?' she asked when they'd found a table.

'To the hospital or to London?'

'Both, I guess.'

'Fine,' he said. 'The staff all seem really nice here, and I trained in London so I feel pretty much at home in the city.'

'That's good.'

There was a slightly awkward silence, as if she didn't really know what to say to him next. It might be easier to keep the conversation going, Leo thought, if he asked her to tell him more about Paddington Children's Hospital and its predicament.

'Obviously Robyn told me about the Board of Directors and their plans, when she asked me to come and work here,' he said, 'so I understand why we're so short-staffed at the moment. But I gather there was a fire at a local school which made things a bit trickier?'

She nodded. 'It was about a month ago. The fire started in the art department, apparently. I'm not sure if it was a broken heater or something that caused the initial fire, but some of the paper caught light.'

'And everything else in an art department tends to be on the flammable side,' he said.

'Exactly. It was pretty scary. The school did what they could to get the kids out, but we were overflowing with patients suffering from everything from smoke inhalation to burns. Simon Bennett had severe facial burns; he's due for some reconstruction surgery, so he's in and out for check-ups at the moment, poor lamb.' She winced. 'And then there's little Ryan.'

'Ryan?' he asked.

'Ryan Walker. He was one of the last to be rescued. The poor little lad was hiding in a cupboard. He heard the firemen when they'd put the fire out in his classroom and came out of the cupboard, but then a beam snapped and hit him on the head.'

'He's lucky to be alive, then,' Leo said.

She nodded. 'But the poor little mite was very badly hurt. He had a craniectomy the other day. Right now he's under sedation and has a helmet on to protect him until the surgical team can replace the skull flap.'

'Poor kid,' Leo said.

'I know. But just think—if we'd been moved to Riverside,' she said softly, 'he wouldn't have made it. And the same's true for Simon.'

'So you're fighting for the hospital to be saved.'

'Victoria's set up a committee—actually, Quinn, Simon's foster mum, is on the committee. We've got protestors outside the gates twenty-four-seven. Though you already know that,' she said. 'You were photographed with them yesterday.'

And the photographs had since been used all round the globe. 'Might as well make the press do something useful,' he said dryly.

'Do the press hound you all the time?' she asked.

'Off and on. It depends if it's a slow news day—but they're rather more interested in the Duke than in the doctor.' He paused. 'Is that why you said about a castle yesterday?'

'Castle?' She frowned for a moment, and then her expression cleared. 'It's what all the staff call the hospital, because of the turrets.'

'Oh.'

She stared at him, looking slightly shocked. 'Hang on. You thought I was having a dig about you being a duke?'

'We didn't exactly get off on the right foot together yesterday,' he pointed out.

'No—and I guess I was a bit rude to you. Sorry.'

He appreciated the apology, though he noticed she didn't give him any explanation about why she'd been so abrupt with him.

'For the record,' he said, 'I did grow up in a castle. And I can tell you it's not all it's cracked up to be. For starters, castles tend to be draughty and full of damp.'

'And full of suits of armour?'

He smiled. 'We do have an armoury, yes. And I have been thinking about opening the place to the public.' Which might give his mother something more immediate to concentrate on, instead of when her son was going to make a suitable marriage and produce an heir to the dukedom.

'But I really don't understand,' she said, 'why a duke would want to be a doctor. I mean, don't you have to do loads of stuff for the dukedom?'

'I delegate a fair bit of it,' he said, 'and I have good staff.'

'Which again makes you different from any other doctor I've met.'

He wondered: was that different good, or different bad?

'I don't know anyone who has staff,' she said. 'Anyone at all. In fact, I don't even know anyone who hires a cleaner.'

'Guilty there, too,' he said. 'Obviously I know

how to use a vacuum cleaner, but there are a lot of other things I'd much rather do with my free time.'

She said nothing.

'I want to be a doctor,' he said softly, 'because I want to make a real difference in the world.'

'Can't you do that as a duke?'

'Not in the same way. I don't want to just throw money at things. It's not enough. I want to make the difference *myself.*'

'From the way you talk,' she said, 'anyone would think you don't actually like being a duke.'

He didn't.

'Let's just say it's not what everyone thinks it would be like—and plenty of people see the title first and not the man.'

She reached out and squeezed his hand in a gesture of sympathy. His hand tingled where her skin touched his, shocking him; he was used to being attracted to women, but he wasn't used to having such a strong reaction to someone and he wasn't quite sure how to deal with it.

She looked as shocked as he felt, as if she'd experienced the same unexpected pull. 'Sorry. I didn't...' Her words trailed off.

Didn't what? Didn't mean to touch him? Or didn't expect to feel that strong a physical reaction?

He had the feeling that she'd find an excuse to run if he called her on it. 'No need to apologise. It's nice that you understand,' he said. 'So have you been working at *this* castle very long?'

'For nearly a year,' she said.

'Where were you before?'

'The other side of London, where I trained.'

He noticed that she hadn't actually said where. Why was so she cagey about her past?

He'd back off, for now. Until he'd got his head round this weird reaction to her and had made sense of it. And then maybe he'd be able to work out what he wanted to do about it. About *her*.

On Wednesday lunchtime, Rosie disappeared, and Leo remembered what Kathleen had said to him: Rosie read to Penny every other day, when she was in. Not quite able to keep himself away, he found himself in the corridor outside Penny's room. Rosie's voice was clear and measured as she read the story, and every so often he could hear a soft giggle of delight from Penny.

'Rosie's so lovely with her,' a voice said beside him.

He looked round; the woman standing next to him looked so much like Penny that there was only one person she could be. 'You're Penny's mum, yes?'

'Julia.'

'Dr Marchetti,' he said, holding out his hand to shake hers. 'Although your daughter isn't one of my patients because I'm not a heart specialist, I work with Rosie, and Rosie told me all about Penny.'

'Rosie's such a lovely woman. So patient. And it's so kind of her to read to Penny in her lunch break.'

'I think you'd probably have a queue of staff there, if you asked,' Leo said. 'From what I hear, Penny's a firm favourite. And her kitten pictures are pinned up in the staff room—they're adorable.'

'Aren't they just?' But behind her smile Julia's eyes were sad. 'I'm sorry, I'm probably keeping you from a patient.'

'It's fine,' Leo reassured her. 'But if there's anything you need?'

'Rosie's there,' Julia said. 'But thank you.'

'I'll let you get on.' He smiled at her, and headed back to his office to prepare for his next clinic. But all the same he couldn't get Rosie out of his head.

Thomas propped himself against the desk where Rosie was sitting. 'Obviously I've read the file, but you've seen Penny more than anyone else this week. How do you feel she's doing?'

Rosie grimaced. 'There doesn't seem to be any change in her condition this week, even though we've been juggling her meds as you asked us to do.'

'So it's not working. I'm beginning to think that the only way forward for her now is a transplant.' He sighed. 'Julia's in today, isn't she? I'll ask her to get Peter to come in as well, so I can talk to them together.'

It wasn't going to be an easy conversation, Rosie knew. 'Do you want me to be there when you talk to them?'

He shook his head. 'Thanks for the offer. I know you've been brilliant with them, but this is my responsibility. It's going to come as a shock to them.'

'You know where I am if you change your mind,' she said gently.

'Thanks, Rosie. I appreciate it.'

Thomas looked almost bruised by this, Rosie thought, but he clearly wasn't going to let anyone close enough to support him. She remembered how it had felt when things with Michael had gone so badly wrong, so she wasn't going to push him to confide in her. But it was always good to know that someone could be there for you if you needed that little bit of support. 'Thomas, I'm probably speaking out of turn, but are you OK?'

'Sure.' He gave her an over-bright smile which clearly underlined the fact that he wasn't OK, but he wanted her to back off.

'Uh-huh,' she said. She didn't quite have the nerve to suggest that maybe he could talk to her if he needed a friend. 'I guess I'll see you later, then.'

He nodded, and left the nurses' station.

Rosie hated this situation. Whatever way you looked at it, someone would lose. She really hoped that Penny would get the heart she needed;

though that would also mean that a family would be bereaved, so it kind of felt wrong to wish for a heart. The best of all outcomes would've been if Penny had responded to the drug treatment, but it wasn't to be.

And poor Julia. Rosie could imagine how she'd feel if she was in Julia's place, worried sick about Freddie or Lexi and knowing that they might not be able to get the treatment they needed so badly. Despite the misery of her life with Michael, he had given her the sheer joy of the twins. She had a lot to be thankful for.

But now wasn't the time to dwell on that. She had a clinic to do.

Leo happened to be checking some files at the nurses' station when Rosie walked over. He could see that she looked upset, and the words were out of his mouth before he could stop them. 'Do you want to go for a drink after work and tell me about it?'

She shook her head.

'Don't tell me—a previous engagement?' he asked wryly.

'I'm afraid so.'

'A chat in the ward kitchen, then.'

'Thanks, but I have obs to do.'

'Thirty minutes,' he said, 'and you can take a five-minute break—and I'm not pulling rank, before you start thinking that. You look upset and I'm trying to be supportive, just as I would with any other colleague who looked upset.'

She looked surprised, and then rueful. 'All right. Thirty minutes,' she said. 'Thank you.'

While she was doing her patients' observations, he finished his paperwork and then nipped out briefly to Tony's Trattoria, the place across the street that he'd been told sold decent coffee, to buy two cappuccinos.

He'd half expected Rosie to make some excuse not to see him, but she arrived in the staff kitchen at the same time as he did.

'Thank you.' She smiled as he handed her one of the distinctive paper cups. 'Someone told you about Tony's, then?'

'Decent Italian coffee? Of course—and it's much better than the coffee in the hospital.'

'We have instant cappuccino here in the ward kitchen,' she reminded him, gesturing to the box of powdered sachets.

'That stuff isn't coffee, it's an abomination.' He smiled back at her. 'So are you going to tell me what's wrong?'

Her beautiful blue eyes filled with sadness. 'I was talking to Thomas earlier. It's Penny.'

He frowned. 'What about Penny?'

'We've been juggling her meds all week and it's just not working.' She shook her head in seeming frustration. 'Thomas says we're probably going to have to look at a transplant, so he's going to do an assessment. But even if she's on the list there's no guarantee she'll get a heart. It could be anything from days, to months, or even more than a year before a suitable heart is available, and it feels horrible to wish for a heart for her because it means that another family's lost someone they love.'

'But at least they have the comfort that their loved one has saved a life by donating their organs after death,' he said softly. 'And you're thinking a heart might not arrive in time?'

'You know that one in five cases don't. Those are really big odds, Leo. And she's such a lovely little girl.'

'Hey.' He gave her a hug. Then he wished he

hadn't, because holding her made him want to do more than that. Right at that moment, he wanted to kiss her tears away—and then kiss her again and again, until he'd made her forget her worries.

When he pulled back slightly and looked her in the eye, her pupils were so huge that her vivid blue irises seemed more like a narrow rim. *So she felt it, too.* He looked at her mouth, and ached to find out for himself how soft and sweet it tasted. He shifted his gaze and caught her looking at his mouth, too. Could they? *Should* they?

He was about to give in to the impulse and dip his head to hers when she pulled away. 'Sorry. It's not appropriate to lean on you like that.'

Leo knew she was right. Except he was the one who'd behaved inappropriately. 'The fault's all mine,' he said. 'I guess it's being Italian that makes me—well...'

'Hug people?' she finished.

'Something like that.' But he wasn't ready to let things go. 'Are you sure I can't take you to dinner tonight?'

'I'm sure. Thank you for the offer, but no.'

And yet there was a hint of wistfulness in her

face. He was sure he wasn't just being a delu-
sional, self-absorbed male; but why did she keep
turning him down whenever he asked her out? If
she'd said that she was married, or in a relationship, fair enough. He'd back off straight away.
But she hadn't said that, which made him think
that it was some other reason why she kept saying no. But he could hardly ask anyone else on
the ward without the risk of becoming the centre
of hospital gossip, and he loathed gossip.

Maybe he'd just keep trying and eventually
he'd manage to wear her down. Because he really liked what he'd seen so far of Rosie Hobbes,
and he wanted to get to know her better. And
he wanted to work out why she attracted him so
strongly, what made her different from the usual
women he dated.

'Thanks for the coffee and sympathy,' Rosie said.
'I'd better get on.'

'See you later,' he said.

The problem was, Rosie thought, Leo Marchetti
was actually *nice*. She'd been on ward rounds
with him a couple of times now and she'd seen
that he was lovely with both the kids and their

parents. A couple of the mums had tried to flirt with him, but he'd stayed totally professional and focused on the children. And he'd been especially good with the more worried parents, explaining things in a way that stopped them panicking.

She was tempted to take him up on his offer of dinner out. Really tempted.

Except she wasn't in the market for a relationship, and it wouldn't be fair to date anyone until she was ready to trust her heart again. And nothing could really happen between her and Leo. He was a duke and moved in the kind of social circles that would never see her as his equal; and, after her experiences with Michael, she refused to put herself in a position where anyone would treat her as second class. It couldn't work, so there was no point in thinking about it. Besides, she already had the perfect life: two gorgeous children, a brilliantly supportive family and a job she adored. Wanting more—wanting a partner to share that with—was just being greedy.

Plus, her judgement was rubbish when it came to men. She'd fallen hook, line and sinker for every lie that Michael had told her.

So she needed to keep thinking of Leo as just another colleague. Yes, he was attractive; and she was beginning to like him a lot. But that was as far as it could go.

CHAPTER THREE

ON FRIDAY MORNING, Leo was talking to Rebecca Scott, the transplant surgeon, on the ward. 'Rosie tells me that Thomas is putting Penny on the transplant list.'

Was it his imagination, or did Rebecca freeze for a second when he mentioned Thomas's name? Rebecca and Thomas were always very professional with patients, but he'd noticed that they never shared a smile or any personal comments with each other, the way they did with other staff members. He had a feeling that something was definitely going on—or maybe something had happened in the past.

He knew all about complicated relationships. He was careful to keep his own as simple as possible, so the women he dated didn't have any expectations that he wouldn't be able to live up to. But, whatever the differences were between Rebecca and Thomas, it was none of his business. As long as everyone on the team was kept informed about any issues with their patients, nothing else mattered. He needed to keep out of this.

'Yes.' There was a flicker of sadness in her eyes, quickly masked. 'Are you settling in to the hospital OK?'

'Yes, thanks.' Clearly Rebecca wanted to change the subject. Well, that was fine by him. The last thing he wanted to do was accidentally trample over a sore spot. 'Everyone's been very welcoming and I haven't had to sit in a corner on my own at lunchtime.'

She smiled. 'That's good. Well, I'm due in Theatre, so I'll let you get on. But give me a yell if there's anything you need.'

'Thanks. I will.'

Rosie spent her usual Friday lunchtime reading to Penny and talking about kittens and ballet. She knew Thomas had talked to Peter and Julia about putting their daughter on the transplant list, and gave Julia an extra hug at the door. 'We're all rooting for her, you know. We're not supposed to have favourites but our Penny's special.'

A tear trickled down Julia's cheek and she clearly couldn't speak.

'It's OK,' Rosie said softly. 'I'm a mum, too, so I know exactly how I'd feel in your shoes.'

'We really appreciate you reading to her,' Julia said.

Rosie smiled back. 'No problem. My two are more into dinosaurs than anything else at the moment, but when Lexi's older I'm sure she'd enjoy the kind of stories I've been reading to Penny.'

In the middle of the afternoon, she was at the nurses' station, writing up notes, when Leo came over and handed her a paper cup of cappuccino. 'Good afternoon. I brought you something to help you write up your notes,' he said.

'That's really nice of you, Leo, and I love the coffee from Tony's,' she said, 'but that's the second time you've bought me coffee this week and now I feel in your debt. Which makes me feel uncomfortable.'

'There's no debt.' He paused. 'Or maybe you

could buy me a coffee after work, if that would make you feel better.'

Buying him a coffee to make them even would make her feel better, but she absolutely couldn't do anything after work. 'Sorry. I can't.'

'Or come out with me for a pizza at the weekend,' he suggested. 'We can go halves and you can buy me a coffee then.'

How easy it would be to agree to have dinner with him.

And it worried Rosie just how much she was starting to like Leo Marchetti. He was kind, he was great with patients and parents and staff alike, and he was beautiful to look at with those dark, expressive eyes and a mouth that promised sin.

It would be so, so easy to say yes.

But how did she know that she wasn't going to be repeating her past mistake and fall for someone who made her heart beat faster but would let her down when she needed him? Leo seemed a nice guy on the ward—but would he be different in a relationship that wasn't strictly professional? Would he turn out to have feet of clay?

There was one way to find out. She could agree

to one date. Then, if Leo took one look at the twins and ran for the hills, she'd know she'd been right about him all along. And she was pretty sure that he would leave her alone once he knew she was a single mum of three-year-old twins.

'All right,' she said. 'But, as you've been buying me coffee, *I'll* take *you* out for a pizza.'

He blinked, looking slightly shocked that she'd actually said yes. 'When?'

'Tomorrow night.' Before her nerve broke.

'OK. That's good. I'll pick you up,' he said. 'What time?'

She frowned. 'Hang on. I thought I was taking you out for pizza? Shouldn't I be the one picking you up?'

'Change of plan. I'm taking you out for dinner,' he said.

So once she'd agreed to something, then he changed the goalposts? Well, Leo would find out the hard way that her goalposts weren't changeable. Her children came first. And that wasn't negotiable.

'Six o'clock, then,' she said, and wrote down her address for him.

'And your phone number? In case of emergencies and change of plans?'

She wrote that down, too.

'Thanks. I'll text you later so you have my number.'

'OK.'

'I'll let you get on,' he said. But before he walked away, he touched the back of his fingers briefly against her cheek—and every nerve-end sizzled at his touch. Just like Wednesday afternoon, when he'd hugged her and then he'd been at the point of actually kissing her. Worse still, she'd been thinking along the same lines.

This really wasn't good.

Rosie had to force herself to concentrate on the paperwork until the end of her shift, and then she headed down to the hospital nursery school to pick up the twins. Right at that moment, she wasn't sure if she'd just made a huge mistake in suggesting going out to dinner with Leo.

But it would settle things once and for all: she was pretty sure he'd look at the twins, make some charming excuse and scuttle off. And then he'd never ask her for another date. She'd be off the hook.

* * *

Leo could hardly believe that Rosie had actually agreed to a date.

Six o'clock seemed a little early for him to pick her up, but maybe they could go for a drink before they went out to dinner. He caught Robyn at the end of his shift. 'Just the person I wanted to see.'

'Something you need at work?' she asked.

He smiled. 'No—everything's fine and I'm really enjoying working here. This is personal. I was wondering if you could recommend a nice restaurant locally.'

'Oh, is your mother coming over to stay?'

He shook his head. 'Right now Mamma's a little frail, so I'd rather she stayed in Tuscany where she can be looked after properly.' He squished the faint feeling of guilt that really he ought to be the one keeping an eye on his mother, as her only child and a qualified doctor. But he specialised in paediatrics, not geriatrics, so she was getting better care than he could give her. And he called her every day when he wasn't in Tuscany; he wasn't neglecting her completely.

'So do you mean somewhere romantic?' Robyn teased.

He actually felt himself blush. 'Yes.'

She mentioned a couple of places and he made a note of them on his phone.

'Dare I ask who the lucky woman is?'

He smiled at her. 'Now, now. A gentleman doesn't tell tales.'

She laughed. 'Leo, you might be a gentleman, but you'll date her twice and be utterly charming, and then you'll end it before she has a chance to get close to you.'

'I date women more than twice,' he said. He knew she was teasing, but he also knew that she had a point. He never had let a woman close to him, since Emilia. Maybe he ought to leave Rosie well alone.

The problem was, he didn't want to. She drew him, with that odd mixture of warmth and wariness. He wanted to get to know her better and understand why she drew him like this. And, if he was honest with himself, she was the first woman since Emilia who'd made him feel this way. Which was another reason why he should just drop this: the last time he'd felt that incredible pull towards someone, it had gone badly wrong.

When he got home, he booked the table at one of the restaurants Robyn had suggested. But, the next day, he couldn't settle to much; he was too filled with anticipation. It made him feel a bit like a teenager again, though the teenage Leo Marchetti had ended up with a heart so broken that he'd had to escape from Rome to London before he could mend himself. He'd never want to go through his teens again, with all that uncertainty and that desperation to please someone who constantly changed the goalposts and made the young Leo feel that he'd never be able to match up to expectations. And he didn't have to ask anyone's permission to date someone.

He shook himself. His father was dead and Leo was comfortable in his own skin now. He knew who he was and what he was good at—and he didn't have to please anyone but himself.

Late that afternoon, he drove to Rosie's and parked his low-slung two-seater convertible on the road outside her house.

She answered the door wearing understated make-up and a little black dress: very different from how she usually was at work, with no make-up and a uniform.

'You look lovely,' he said, and then felt like a fool when she raised one eyebrow.

'Not that you don't usually look lovely,' he said, feeling even more gauche. Which was weird, because normally he was relaxed with women. He *liked* their company. Why was he so awkward with Rosie?

She smiled. 'Thank you for the compliment. Come in.'

He stopped dead in the doorway when she ushered him into the living room and he saw two small children playing with a train set on the floor. The brown-haired boy and golden-haired girl were clearly Rosie's children, as they had her bright blue eyes and her smile. And they looked to be around the same age, so he guessed that they were twins.

He couldn't see a babysitter anywhere, unless maybe someone was in the kitchen or something.

And the penny dropped when he looked at Rosie's face.

She'd invited him to pick her up here, expecting him to take one look at the children and make a run for it.

That really smarted. Had his reputation already spread through the hospital, if she thought he was that shallow?

Then again, maybe she'd been badly hurt by the twins' father. Until he knew the full story, he shouldn't judge her the way she'd obviously misjudged him.

'So that's dinner for four?' he asked.

She shrugged, and lowered her voice so the children couldn't hear. 'I come as a package, Leo.'

'It would've been useful to know that.'

'So you could back off earlier?'

She was really that sure he was so unreliable? Or had someone made her believe that about all men? 'No,' he said. 'So I could've brought a four-seater car with me instead of a two-seater.'

Colour flooded into her face. 'Oh.'

'I would be delighted to take you all out,' he said, keeping his voice as low as hers, 'but either we need to use a taxi or—if you have appropriate seats—your car. Is there any particular place the children like eating out?'

* * *

Leo wasn't running away.

And he'd asked where the twins liked eating out, not where she liked eating out.

He was putting her children first.

Shame flooded through Rosie. She'd misjudged him. Badly so. Every single assumption she'd made about him had been based on Michael's behaviour, and that wasn't fair of her. OK, so the hospital grapevine said Leo dated a lot, but she hadn't heard anything about him leaving a trail of broken hearts behind him. It was possible to be good-looking and be a decent human being as well. She knew her experiences with Michael had made her unfairly judgemental, but it was so hard not to just leap in and make assumptions.

'Thank you,' she said, feeling like an ungrateful monster. 'Are you sure about this?'

'The children are obviously dressed up, ready to go out,' he said. 'I'm not going to disappoint them.'

'I said I'd take them out,' she admitted.

'So how were you going to explain me to them?'

'You're my colleague. You popped in to tell me something about the hospital, and you couldn't come for a pizza with us because you're already due somewhere else.'

He raised an eyebrow. 'So you really did think I'd take one look at the children and scuttle away.'

'Yes, and I apologise. I was wrong to judge you on someone else's behaviour.' She closed her eyes briefly. 'I'll explain later, but I'd prefer not to discuss it in front of the twins.'

'All right. So shall I cancel our table while you book us a table somewhere that the twins like?'

This was way, way more than she deserved. 'Thank you,' she said. She'd already booked the table; but, sure that he wouldn't join them, she'd booked it for three rather than for four. It wouldn't take much to change that. 'And I'm sorry.'

Leo said nothing, just gave her a grave little nod that made her feel about two inches tall.

Leo walked back into the hallway and called the restaurant to cancel his booking. Once he'd ended the connection, he waited for Rosie to finish her own call, then followed her into the living room and crouched down to the twins' level. 'Hello. I'm Leo.'

The little boy refused to look at him, but the girl smiled at him. 'I'm Lexi. My name starts with a *luh*, like yours.'

'Delighted to meet you, Lexi.' He shook her hand, then looked at the little boy. 'And you are…?'

The little boy dipped his head and looked up shyly.

He had Rosie's eyes, Leo thought, huge and piercing and beautiful.

'He's Freddie,' Lexi said.

Did he always let his sister do the talking for him? Leo wondered. 'Delighted to meet you, too, Freddie,' he said, and held out his hand.

But the little boy looked wary and refused to take his hand.

Was Freddie wary of all men, or just of him? Leo wondered. Given that there was no evidence of the twins' father, had there been some kind of super-bitter divorce? It would perhaps explain why Rosie had been so quick to judge him harshly—and maybe the twins' father was the person she'd referred to when she'd talked about judging Leo on someone else's behaviour.

'I work with your mummy at the hospital,' he said.

'We go to school at the hospital,' Lexi said.

'School?' They looked a bit young to be at school.

'Nursery school,' Rosie explained.

That made a lot of sense. Now he understood why she rushed off at the end of every shift and had consistently refused to meet him after work: she needed to pick up her children straight after work.

'How old are you, Freddie?' he asked.

The little boy said nothing, and Lexi—clearly the more confident of the two—nudged him, as if to say, *Answer the man*.

'Freddie's a little bit shy,' Rosie said.

'Mummy says don't talk to someone you don't know,' Lexi said.

'Quite right,' Leo said.

'But you know Mummy, so we can talk to you,' Lexi added.

'Three,' Freddie said reluctantly. 'I'm three.'

'I'm three and a little bit,' Lexi said. 'I was borned before Freddie.'

Leo had to hide a smile at both her charming

grammatical mistake and the importance of her tone. 'So you're the older twin, Lexi.'

Freddie seemed to have a burst of confidence, because he said, 'Mummy's taking us out. We're having pizza for tea.'

'And I'm going with you,' Leo told him.

'Why?' Lexi asked.

'Lexi, that's rude,' Rosie warned.

'It's fine,' Leo reassured her. 'I'm coming with you because your mummy's very kind. I haven't worked at the hospital for very long and I don't know many people, so she thought I might be lonely this evening and said I could maybe come for pizza with you. If that's all right with you both, Freddie and Lexi?'

The twins looked at each other.

'So Mummy's your friend?' Freddie asked.

'She is,' Leo confirmed, not quite daring to meet Rosie's eyes. Friendship definitely didn't describe their relationship. But it would do for now.

'Then you're our friend, too,' Lexi said. Her smile was so much like Rosie's that it made Leo's heart feel as if it had just flipped over. Given how wary Rosie had been with him, it wouldn't be surprising if her children were just as nervous with people. Yet Lexi had seemed to accept him almost instantly.

'Are you coming to the park with us?' Freddie asked.

'We're not going to the park tonight, Freddie,' Rosie said.

'Tomorrow?' Lexi asked hopefully.

'We'll see. But we need to go for pizza now, so we have to put the trains away.'

Freddie stuck out his lower lip. 'But we want to play trains when we get back.'

'We'll see,' Rosie said. 'For now, we need to put the trains away before we go out. Shall we have a race and see who can put the track away fastest?'

'Me!' Lexi said.

'Me!' Freddie echoed.

Between them, they dismantled the wooden track and put it into a large plastic lidded box. Leo held back, watching them. Rosie was strict with her children rather than spoiling them, insisting that they clear up and have good manners. But he was also pretty sure that Rosie Hobbes would never, ever starve her children of love.

In her case, firm went with fair, and he'd just bet that she told the twins every day—several times—that she loved them.

How different his own childhood had been. His mother had spoiled him but had never stood up for him, and his father had been cold and manipulative, seeing Leo firstly as the future Duke and only secondly as his child. The child who constantly disappointed him.

He pushed the thoughts away. Now wasn't the time to dwell on that.

'Do you mind me driving?' Rosie asked Leo when she'd strapped the children into their car seats.

'No.'

She grimaced. 'Sorry. Judging again. I don't mean to.'

'Any man who has a problem with a woman driving,' Leo said softly, 'needs to get a life.'

Which made her warm to him even more.

The children insisted on singing all the way to the pizza place; Rosie knew she was being a coward by letting it give her the excuse not to make small-talk with Leo, but right now she felt so wrong-footed.

She made each child hold her hand on the way in to the restaurant; once they were seated, with Lexi next to him and Freddie opposite, Leo asked the children, 'So is this your favourite place to eat?'

'Yes! We love pizza,' Lexi said.

'Me, too,' Leo said, 'because I was born in Italy, where pizza comes from.'

'Where's Italy?' Lexi asked.

Rosie was about to head her off, knowing that her daughter could ask a million questions and then a million more, but Leo took out his phone and pulled up a map. 'See that long, thin country there that looks a bit like a boot? That's Italy. And I come from here.' He pointed out a region to the north-west of the country.

Tuscany. The part of Italy Rosie had always wanted to visit. She and Michael had planned a tour of the area, stopping off at Florence and Siena and Pisa—but then he'd had to cancel their holiday because he was starting a new job. More like, she thought grimly, he'd gambled away the money he'd been supposed to use for their flights and hotels, and she'd been too naive to realise. She'd believed every word he'd said.

'Are the houses pretty?' Lexi asked.

'Very pretty.' Leo pulled up some pictures to show her. 'See?'

'That one looks a bit like the hospital,' Lexi said, ''cept it's yellow, not pink.'

'Are there castles in Italy?' Freddie piped up.

'There are castles,' Leo said, and found some more pictures. 'In Italy we call a castle a *palazzo*.'

'Pal—' Freddie began, and stopped.

'Palazzo. Like a palace,' Leo said. *'Pal-at-zo.'*

'Pal-as-o,' Freddie repeated, not quite getting it, but Rosie noticed that Leo didn't push him or mock him. Instead, he was actually encouraging the little boy to talk.

'Are there princesses in the castle?' Lexi asked.

'The waitress is here, Lexi. We need to tell her what we want to eat,' Rosie interrupted gently.

'Dough balls,' Lexi said promptly.

'Dough balls, what?' Rosie reminded her.

'Dough balls, please,' Lexi said.

'Me, too, please,' Freddie said.

'That's three for dough balls, please,' Leo said.

Rosie smiled. 'Four for dough balls, please, two

small *margherita* pizzas for the children, a four cheeses thin crust for me and...' She paused and looked at Leo.

'A *quattro stagioni* thin crust for me, please,' Leo said.

Lexi's eyes went round. 'What's a cat—?' She stopped, looking puzzled.

'*Quattro stagioni,*' Leo said. 'It means "four seasons" in Italian, and each quarter of the pizza has a topping of food you find in each season. Do you know what the seasons are?'

'Like spring,' Rosie prompted when Lexi was uncharacteristically quiet.

Lexi shook her head.

'That's OK,' Leo said. 'Spring's when the daffodils and bluebells come out, summer's when it's hot, autumn's when all the leaves turn gold and fall off the trees, and winter's when it's cold and snowy.'

Of course Leo was good with kids, Rosie thought. He was a paediatrician and spent every working day treating children. It stood to reason that he'd be good with children outside work, too. But she appreciated the way he'd explained the concept simply and without fuss, rather than dismissing Lexi's question or ignoring her.

Lexi continued quizzing Leo about Italy while they were waiting for their meal, and even Freddie started to come out of his shell when Leo started asking him about his favourite trains. He also helped Freddie cut up his pizza without making a big deal of it, and Rosie felt the barrier round her heart start to crack.

This was what she'd always thought having a family would be like.

Except Michael hadn't wanted that. She and the children simply hadn't been enough for him. And OK, she could deal with the fact that maybe he'd made a mistake in choosing her as his life partner; but how could he have turned his back on his children? All this time later, it still hurt.

Leo was used to dealing with children at work, but very few outside. And he was surprised to discover how at ease he felt with chatterbox Lexi and shy Freddie.

Every so often, he glanced across at Rosie, to check that she was comfortable about the way he was chatting with her twins, and he was amazed to see that she actually looked relaxed—something he most definitely wasn't used to seeing from her at work.

Leo didn't do relationships; Robyn's teasing assessment had been very close to the mark. Yet he found himself drawn to this little family. And he was actually enjoying himself, answering Lexi's barrage of questions and trying to tempt Freddie out of his shell.

This was the kind of childhood he wished he'd had. Where his father might have cut up his meals for him without making a big deal about it, rather than making him eat his meals on his own in the nursery until he was old enough to know which knife and fork to use, and use them without spilling anything. Where his mother would have helped him decorate his whipped ice-cream sundae with sprinkles and jelly beans, not minding if anything spilled on the table or on her clothes. Though he had a feeling that she'd been acting on his father's decisions rather than her own; if you were fragile and you were married to a bully, it would be easier to agree with him than to risk a fight.

You couldn't change the past.

But maybe, he thought, his future could be different.

And maybe it didn't mean having to find himself a 'suitable' noble bride and producing an heir to the dukedom. Maybe it was about finding the life and the family that he wanted.

Maybe.

CHAPTER FOUR

AFTER THE MEAL, Rosie drove them back to her house.

It would be rude not to invite Leo in for coffee; but she was pretty sure that he'd make an excuse not to come in. Although he'd been lovely with the children, tonight hadn't been the romantic date for two he'd been expecting, and she wouldn't blame him for feeling just a bit disgruntled with her. When she'd planned this evening, she'd thought it was the best way of making him understand she wasn't interested in a date; but now she could see how stupid and selfish she'd been. She should've just told him straight.

Except a little part of her *had* wanted to date him.

And Leo Marchetti made her feel seriously flustered.

'You're welcome to come in for coffee,' she

said, 'but I quite understand if you need to get going.'

His dark eyes were unreadable. 'Coffee would be lovely, thank you.'

Oh, help. He wasn't rushing away as fast as he possibly could. This felt as if she'd leaped out of the frying pan and into the fire.

'I'll put the kettle on, if you don't mind waiting while I put the children to bed?' she asked as she closed the front door behind them.

'I don't want to go to bed,' Lexi said.

'It's bedtime now, Lexi,' Rosie said firmly. 'And if you want to go to the park tomorrow, you need to get enough sleep tonight. I'll read you a story.'

'I want Leo to read me a story,' Freddie said. 'He's my friend.'

'Leo...' She paused, trying to think up a reasonable excuse.

'—would be delighted to read you a story,' Leo cut in gently. 'Do you have a favourite story, Freddie?'

'Dinosaurs!' Freddie said, and charged up the stairs.

'Thank you,' Rosie mouthed to him.

Once Rosie had brushed the children's teeth and Lexi and Freddie were in their pyjamas, cuddled beneath their duvets, Leo sat on the panda-shaped rug on the floor between their beds, holding the book that Freddie had picked out.

'*One* story,' Rosie said, and kissed them both. 'I'm going to put the kettle on for Leo and me to have coffee. Night-night. I love you, Freddie. I love you, Lexi.'

'Love you, Mummy,' they chorused. 'Night-night.'

In her small galley kitchen, Rosie could hear Leo reading the story. She loved the fact that he actually put on different voices for different dinosaurs; but part of her wanted to cry. This was something the children had really missed out on; although their grandfather often read to them, it wasn't quite the same as having their father read them a bedtime story every night.

Being a parent sometimes felt like the hardest, loneliest job in the world; although her parents and her sister were brilliantly supportive, it wasn't the same as having someone with her all the time. Someone to help make the decisions.

Once Leo finished the story, he sang a lullaby

to them. Rosie didn't recognise the words and was pretty sure that he was singing in Italian, but he had a gorgeous voice. It was something that Michael had never bothered doing, and he'd actually smashed the CD of children's songs she'd bought for the car because he said it annoyed him and he couldn't put up with the twins caterwauling the same song over and over again.

Michael.

She was going to have to tell Leo about Michael. She'd promised him an explanation and she wasn't going to back out; but it wasn't a pretty story and even now she felt sick about how poor her judgement had been.

She busied herself making the coffee until she heard Leo come down the stairs. 'Thank you for reading to them—and for singing a lullaby. That was really kind of you.'

'No problem,' he said. 'They're nice kids.'

'Thank you.' She added milk to her own mug, then handed him the other. 'It's instant,' she warned, 'but it's decent instant coffee.'

'"Decent" instant coffee? I'm not entirely sure there is such a thing,' Leo said with a smile, 'but thank you.' He glanced at the drawings held to the outside of the fridge with magnets. 'I like the pictures.'

'The pink one is Lexi's and the yellow one is Freddie's. They feel about dogs the way that Penny at the hospital feels about kittens,' Rosie said ruefully. 'Nearly all their pictures are of puppies.'

'But you don't have one?'

She shrugged. 'I'd love one. But it wouldn't be fair to leave a dog on its own all day.'

Which was why he didn't have a dog, either. He took a sip of the coffee.

'Is it as bad as you thought it would be?' she asked, looking slightly worried.

Yes. Not that he was going to tell her that. 'It's drinkable.'

'But you'd prefer proper coffee?'

He shrugged and smiled. 'I'm from Tuscany. We Italians take our coffee seriously.'

'I guess.' She looked awkward. 'Well, come through.'

He followed her into the living room. Like her kitchen, it was tiny; yet it was also cosy, and there were photographs of the children on the walls, from what was clearly their very first picture in hospital through to a more recent-looking one that he assumed had been taken at the hospital nursery school.

And there were lumps of clay on the mantelpiece that were clearly meant to be dogs. Leo couldn't remember his parents ever displaying his artwork. Then again, maybe dukes and duchesses weren't supposed to put their young children's very first clay models among the Meissen and Sèvres porcelain.

'I enjoyed tonight,' he said. And he was surprised by how much he had relished the feeling of being part of a normal family.

'I'm afraid the twins can be a bit full-on,' she admitted, 'especially when Lexi starts chattering away. She really could talk the proverbial hind leg off a donkey.'

'She's lovely,' he said, 'and it's good that she's confident.'

'Probably because she's the elder twin—well, by all of fifteen minutes—and girls' language seems to develop faster than that of boys. Though I worry about Freddie,' she said. 'He's so shy.'

'Lots of young children go through a shy

phase.' They could pussyfoot around the subject for ever, or he could push her just a little bit to find out why she'd been so sure he would walk away as soon as he saw the twins. 'Until tonight, I had no idea you had children.'

'Or you would never have asked me out?'

'That isn't what I said.'

'No. Sorry.' She sighed. 'And I'm really sorry I misjudged you. And I misled you. It was wrong of me.'

He might as well ask her outright. 'Who hurt you so badly, Rosie? Who broke your trust?'

She grimaced. 'Michael. My ex.'

'Freddie and Lexi's father?'

She nodded. 'I owe you the truth. But not everyone at work knows the whole story and I'd prefer to keep it that way.'

He could understand that. He didn't exactly tell many people about his own past. 'I won't betray your confidence.'

She looked at him, her eyes a piercing blue; and then she seemed to make the decision to trust him. 'I met Michael at a party when I was twenty-two, a year after I'd finished my nursing training. He was a friend of a friend. I thought he was charming and fun when I met him, and he was the most good-looking man I'd ever met. I couldn't believe it when he actually asked me out. And dating him was like nothing I'd ever experienced before. We went to the most amazing places—Michelin-starred restaurants, VIP seats at concerts for really big-name bands, and he whisked me away to the poshest hotel in Paris for my birthday. He completely swept me off my feet.' She looked away. 'We'd been together for three months when he asked me to marry him. Of course I said yes. I'd fallen in love with the sweetest, most charming man and I could hardly believe that he felt the same way about me. He made me feel so special.'

But obviously things had gone sour.

'And then it wasn't fun any more?' he asked gently.

'He changed,' she said, 'when I fell pregnant— it happened pretty quickly and, although he told me he was thrilled to be a dad, it didn't feel like it. He changed jobs a lot. I thought it was because he was ambitious and wanted to make a good life for our children.'

Leo didn't need to ask for the 'but'.

'He started coming home later and later,' Rosie said. 'And then the bailiffs came round. Michael told me that he was taking care of the bills and the money, and it was my job to take care of the children.' She looked away. 'Except he wasn't actually taking care of the money. I had no idea at the time, but he had a gambling problem. When I finally saw our bank statement, I realised that we were in debt up to our eyeballs.' She took a deep breath. 'Gambling's an illness. I know that. And I believed in my marriage vows, being with him in sickness and in health, so I tried to support him. I found him a group that would help him beat the addiction, and a good counsellor. He promised me he'd go. That he'd stop gambling. For our children's sake.'

And it was very clear to Leo that Michael had broken that promise.

'The next time someone came round demanding money,' Rosie said softly, 'it wasn't a bailiff. Michael was in debt to—I don't know any names, but they definitely weren't the kind of people you'd want to cross. All the time I thought he was going to counselling and the support group, it turned out he was still gambling and getting into more and more debt. He'd bailed out of the support group and the counselling after the very first session. And this man...' She shuddered. 'He threatened the children. His eyes looked dead, Leo. He meant it. If Michael didn't pay the money he owed, something would happen to the children. That man looked at them as if they were just leverage, not precious little lives. There was no pity, no compassion. I've never been so scared in my life.'

'Couldn't the police protect you and the children?'

She shook her head. 'This guy didn't act as if he was afraid of the law. I threatened to call the police. He just looked at me, and he didn't need to say a word: I knew that if I reached for the phone he'd break every bone in my hands to stop me. And then probably a few more to teach me a lesson.' She grimaced. 'He said Michael had three days to pay up, or else.'

'And you didn't go to the police?'

'I did, the very second he left, but I had no evidence. I couldn't describe the man in detail, I didn't know any names, and Michael wasn't talking. And I was so scared, Leo. Not for me, but for my babies. They were only two years old, still toddlers. I couldn't risk anything happening to them.' She closed her eyes. 'I could have forgiven Michael for lying to me—but I couldn't forgive him for putting our babies in danger. I asked him why he didn't go to the support group or to counselling. He said he didn't want to. And you can't change someone, Leo. If they don't want to change, you can nag and nag and nag until you're blue in the face—and all you'll do is give yourself a headache because they won't listen or do anything different. I told him I was leaving with the children, and as he'd clearly chosen gambling over us I was going to divorce him so I could keep them safe. My parents were brilliant. They took us in until I found my job at the Castle and this flat, and could get back on my own two feet.'

'And you divorced Michael and the thugs never came back?'

She blew out a breath. 'That's the bit I regret. The bit where I think maybe I should've done more. Because he died before I could even get an appointment with the solicitor,' she said. 'He was in a car accident.'

Something in her expression told him that there

was more to it than that. 'But you don't think it was an accident?'

'I don't know. He was the only one involved. Michael, a tree and a soft-top car that I found out later was about to get repossessed because he hadn't kept up the payments.' She bit her lip. 'That man said he had three days to pay up. And the accident happened the day after the deadline.'

'So you think the bad guys had something to do with it?'

'I don't have any proof. I don't know if the people he owed money to decided to make an example of him for anyone else who thought about not paying them back, or whether Michael knew he'd run out of options and he drove straight into the tree because he couldn't see any other way out of the mess he'd made. Either way, I know I should've done more to help him. The crash was on a little country road and it was hours before anyone found him.' She looked haunted. 'His legs were shattered in the crash, and he bled out. He died all on his own, Leo, thinking everything was hopeless.'

'It wasn't your fault that he died, Rosie,' Leo said. 'You tried to get him to go to counselling.

You found him a support group. He chose not to go. He lied to you about it, he got into even more debt with the wrong kind of people and he put the children at risk. You can't be responsible for someone else's choices.'

'What he did was wrong, but he didn't deserve to die for it.' She dragged a hand through her hair, looking weary. 'I told the police everything I knew, but there wasn't any evidence to back it up. And the people he owed money to haven't come after me, so I guess they must have decided that his death cleared his debt.'

'Do you see anything of Michael's family?'

She shook her head. 'He fell out with them before he met me. They didn't come to the wedding, even though we invited them. They've never even seen the twins.' She swallowed hard. 'And they didn't come to Michael's funeral.'

'It must've been a really bad row.' Despite his differences with his own father, Leo had attended the funeral. He'd even sat by his father's hospital bed for twenty-four hours straight after the first stroke, hoping that they might have some kind of reconciliation and he could help his father towards recovery. But the elder Leo had been intractable, and they hadn't reconciled properly before the second—fatal—stroke.

He still felt guilty, as if he could've done more. So he understood exactly where Rosie was coming from. And he wasn't sure if it was more a need to give or receive comfort that made him put his arms round her.

That first touch undid him even more than the first time when he'd hugged her and almost kissed her. This time, the impulse was way too strong to resist.

He could feel the warmth of her body through the material of her dress and his shirt, and it made him want more. He knew he shouldn't be doing this, but he couldn't help dipping his head and brushing his lips against hers. His mouth tingled where it touched hers, and warmth slid all the way down his spine.

Rosie was still for a moment, as if shocked that he'd made such a bold move—but then, just when he was about to pull away and apologise, she slid her hand round his neck and kissed him back. It felt as if fireworks were going off inside his head.

When he finally broke the kiss, her cheeks were flushed and her mouth was reddened and full. He had a feeling that he looked in the same kind of state.

'Sorry,' he said. 'I shouldn't have done that.'

She stroked his face. 'It wasn't just you,' she said wryly.

'So what are we going to do about this?' he asked. 'I like you, Rosie.'

'I like you, too,' she admitted.

There was a 'but'. He could see it in her expression.

'But we can't do this,' she said softly. 'Right now I'm focused on my children and my career.'

'That's totally understandable,' he said. She was a single mum. Of course her children had to come first.

'And you're only here on a temporary contract. I guess you'll be going back to Italy when it's over.'

'Maybe, maybe not.' He shrugged. 'My plans are quite fluid at the moment.'

She frowned. 'But you have commitments in Italy. You're a duke.'

'And, as I told you the other day, I delegate a lot of the work. I have excellent staff.'

'But at the end of the day you're still the Duke,

and you have responsibilities,' she said. 'I imagine you'll have to marry some European princess.'

'Not necessarily a princess,' he said.

'But not a commoner.'

'That was a sticking point for my father,' he said—and then was horrified to realise what he'd just blurted out.

This dismay must've shown on his face, because she took his hand and squeezed it. 'Don't worry. I'm not going to spread that round the hospital or rush out to spill the beans to the first paparazzo I can find.'

'Thank you.' And he believed she'd keep his confidence, the way he'd keep hers.

'Considering what I just told you,' she said, 'if you ever want to talk…'

'Thank you.' Though he had no intention of telling her about his past. About Emilia, the girl he'd fallen in love with in his first week at university—and how his father had disapproved of Emilia's much poorer background. Leo hadn't realised it at the time, but his father had made life hard for her behind the scenes; his father had pulled strings and made it clear that he'd ruin her

life if she didn't stop seeing Leo. Emilia had resisted for a while, but in the end she'd broken up
with Leo. And she'd left university, too; he hadn't
been able to track her down.

He'd learned the hard way that 'love conquers
all' wasn't true. He'd loved Emilia and she'd loved
him, but it hadn't been enough to overcome his
father's opposition. And Leo hadn't been pre-
pared to settle for an arranged marriage without
love, or to bring a child into the dysfunctional
world he'd grown up in. He wanted to change
things. To make a difference to the world. To do
good. And so he, too, had left the university at
Rome, and applied to read medicine in London.
His father had threatened to disown him, and by
that point Leo had stopped caring about trying to
please someone who could never, ever be pleased.
He'd simply smiled and said, 'Do it.'

His father hadn't disowned him.

And Leo had still been stuck with the dukedom.

'Tell me,' she said softly.

He shook his head. 'Old news. And you can't
change the past. I've come to terms with it.'

'Have you?'

'Probably not.' He couldn't stop himself running the pad of his thumb along her lower lip, and his whole body tightened when her beautiful blue eyes went dark with the same desire that flooded through him. 'What are we going to do about this thing between us?'

'I don't know. Pretend it isn't happening, I guess,' she said. 'I have to put the children first.'

'Agreed.'

'And you're probably not going to be around for long. I can't bring you into their lives, only for you to leave as soon as they get attached to you. I won't do that to them.'

It was so easy to break a child's heart. He knew that one first-hand and still had the scars from it. 'So see me when they're not around.'

'I'm a single mum, Leo. When I'm not at work, I'm with them all the time.'

'And at work we're both busy. I won't ask you to give up your lunchtimes reading to Penny. That wouldn't be fair to anyone.'

'So we're colleagues.' She paused. 'Maybe friends.'

That wasn't enough. 'I want to see you, Rosie,' he said softly. 'There has to be a way. Tell the children what you told them today—that I'm new at work and don't know many people at the hospital. That's true.'

She was silent for so long that he thought she was going to say no. Then she grimaced. 'Leo, I'm not very good at relationships.'

Neither was he.

'I find it hard to trust,' she admitted.

Given what she'd told him about her ex, that was understandable. 'I don't have any easy answers,' he said, not wanting to brush her feelings aside and make her feel that she was making a fuss over nothing. But he didn't want to make some glib, smooth reply, either. 'I have no idea where this is going. But I like you, Rosie, and I think you might like me. So isn't it worth a try?'

Again, she was silent while she thought about it. Finally, she nodded. 'As far as the children are concerned, you're *just* my friend from work. My friend who isn't going to be around for very long.'

'That's fair.' He paused. 'And when they're asleep… Then I get to hold your hand. To talk to you. To kiss you.'

She went very pink, and Leo couldn't resist

stealing another kiss. Rosie Hobbes, now she was letting him a little closer, was utterly adorable.

'It's Sunday tomorrow,' she said, and Leo loved the fact that her voice had gone all breathy.

'So we can do something together, the four of us?'

'The park, maybe,' she suggested.

'That sounds good. Shall I pick you up or meet you there?'

'Meet us there,' she said. 'Half-past ten. I'll text you the postcode so you can find it on your satnav.'

'OK.' He stole another kiss. 'I'm going now. While I can still be on my best behaviour.'

The colour in her face deepened, and he guessed that she was wondering what it would be like if he wasn't on his best behaviour; even the thought of it made him feel hot and bothered.

'Tomorrow,' he said.

But on Sunday morning, when Leo was showering after his usual early-morning run, he realised how selfish he was being.

He'd let his attraction to Rosie get in the way of his common sense.

She was absolutely right. They shouldn't do this. She needed to put her children first. It wasn't fair for him to let her and the children get close to him, then walk away. She needed more than he could offer her—more than a fling. What did he know about a normal family life? This wasn't fair to any of them. He needed to do the right thing and call a halt.

As soon as he was dressed and his coffee was brewing, he texted her.

Sorry. Can't make it.

And hopefully by the time he saw her at work tomorrow he'd have a reasonable excuse lined up.

Sorry. Can't make it.

Rosie stared at the message on her phone.

So Leo had changed his mind about going to the park with her and the children. He hadn't even given a polite excuse, saying that he was needed at work or there was a family thing he had to sort out; he'd sent just a plain and simple statement that he wasn't coming.

So she'd been right to be wary of trusting him.

OK, he hadn't bolted on seeing the twins and he'd even been really sweet with them, reading them a bedtime story and singing them a lullaby. But now he'd had time to think about it and clearly he'd realised that she wasn't what he wanted. She wasn't able to give him a simple, uncomplicated relationship; she came with baggage and a heap of mistrust. Plus, they came from such different worlds: he was the heir to a dukedom and she was a single mum of two. With all that, how could it possibly work?

She shouldn't have let down her guard last night. But instead she'd told him everything about Michael—and she'd let him kiss her.

What a fool she'd been.

Well, she'd still take the children to the park. They weren't going to miss out on a treat just because she'd been so foolish.

Tomorrow, when she had to face Leo at work, she'd act as if nothing had happened. And she'd keep him at a distance for the rest of his time at Paddington Children's Hospital.

CHAPTER FIVE

ON MONDAY MORNING, Rosie kissed Freddie and Lexi goodbye at the hospital nursery school. 'See you after work,' she said with a smile.

'Are we going to have pizza with Leo tonight?' Freddie asked.

'No.'

Nina, the children's favourite classroom assistant, raised an eyebrow. 'Who's Leo?'

Oh, help, Rosie thought. Still, at least she was here when the subject was raised—and now she could make it very clear that the man the twins had adored when he'd met them on Saturday was absolutely not going to be a fixture in their lives. 'He's a new colleague,' Rosie said. 'You know what it's like when you start a new job and you don't know anyone. There's nothing worse than being all alone on a Saturday night, so I invited him to join us for pizza.'

'Uh-huh.' Nina didn't look the slightest bit convinced.

Rosie definitely didn't want this turning into hospital gossip. 'I think he has a soft spot for one of the nurses in the Emergency Department,' she said. It wasn't true, but she hadn't been specific so it wasn't *quite* the same as spreading a rumour. She was just deflecting the attention from herself. 'So now—thanks to the twins—he knows a nice pizza place to take someone to.'

'Right,' Nina said, still not looking completely convinced.

'My shift starts in five minutes. I need to go,' Rosie said, kissed the twins goodbye again and left before Nina could quiz her any further.

And of course the first person she saw when she walked onto the ward *would* have to be Leo Marchetti.

The man she'd thought would run a mile, but had surprised her.

The man who'd sung a lullaby to her children, then kissed her until her knees had gone weak.

The man who'd then changed his mind and lived all the way down to her original expectations.

'Dr Marchetti,' she said, and gave him a cool nod.

'Ros—' he began but, at her even cooler stare, he amended his words to, 'Nurse Hobbes.'

Worse still, she discovered that she was working in the allergy clinic with him all day.

Well, she could be professional. She could work with the man and make sure that their patients had the best possible care. And she'd make quite sure that all their conversations revolved around their patients.

'Our first patient is Madison Turner,' she said. 'She's six, had anaphylactic shock after being stung by a wasp, and this is her second appointment for venom immunotherapy. Two weeks ago, she had six injections over the course of a day and she responded well.'

'Good. So today she's due for three injections,' Leo said. 'Would you like to bring her in?'

'Of course, Dr Marchetti.' By the end of today, Rosie was sure she'd be sick to the back teeth of being polite and professional, but she'd do it for the sake of their patients. And she'd be very glad when her shift was over.

When she brought Madison and her mother

in, Leo smiled at them and introduced himself. 'Good morning. You already know Nurse Hobbes. I'm Dr Marchetti—Dr Leo, if you prefer.'

'Good morning,' Mrs Turner said.

'Hello, Dr Leo,' Madison said shyly.

'Before we start, can I just check that you have your emergency kit with you,' Rosie asked, 'and that Madison had her antihistamines last night?'

'We did everything you said in your letter,' Mrs Turner confirmed.

'That's great. So how have you been doing since you came in last?' Leo asked Madison.

The little girl looked at her mum, who smiled and said, 'She's been fine. No problems. Her hay fever flared up a bit on the day we came here last, but Rosie had already told us to expect it and everything was fine after that.'

'Good. Today's going to be very similar to last time, except Madison will only have three injections instead of six,' Leo explained. 'We'll space them an hour apart, but we'd like you to stay in the department for an hour or so after she has the last one, so we can keep an eye on her in case of any allergic reactions.'

Mrs Turner patted her bag. 'We have books and a games console,' she said, 'plus drinks and snacks—nothing with nuts, in case someone else is allergic to them.'

'That's perfect,' Rosie said with a smile. 'If everything's OK today, we'll see you for a single injection next month, and then a monthly maintenance dose. Madison, Dr Leo needs to have a quick look at you and I need to take a few measurements and get you to blow into a tube for me—that's to check how your breathing is, so we're happy you're fine to have your next treatment. Is that OK?'

The little girl nodded, and between them Leo examined her and Rosie took all the obs and did a lung function test. 'Everything's fine,' she confirmed to Leo.

'Nurse Hobbes has some special cream so the injection won't be so sore,' Leo said, and Rosie used the anaesthetic cream to numb the injection site on Madison's skin.

'Mrs Turner, if Madison has any kind of allergy symptoms between now and the next injection, we'd like you to tell us straight away,' Leo said. 'I realise you probably already know them, but

I like to be clear so I'll repeat them, if you don't mind. If Madison has a rash or any itching, if she feels dizzy or light-headed or generally not very well, if there's any swelling of her face, lips or tongue, if it's hard for her to breathe or if her heartbeat's too fast, then we need to know right away.'

'Got it,' Mrs Turner said.

'Madison, can you look at the butterfly on the ceiling and count the spots for me?' Leo asked, and swiftly administered the injection before she'd finished counting.

'Seven,' Madison said.

He smiled at her. 'Good girl. Thank you. We'll see you in an hour.'

Rosie followed the Turners out to the waiting room. 'Let us know if you're worried about any-thing,' she said. 'And you might find that, just like last time, Madison's hay fever is a little bit worse tonight, but an antihistamine will help.'

'We're prepared for that, thanks to you,' Mrs Turner said. 'No hot baths tonight, either, and we need to just have a very quiet and lazy eve-ning, right?'

'Right,' Rosie confirmed with a smile.

* * *

Leo noticed that Rosie was being super-professional with him. She only spoke to him when necessary between patients, and kept popping out to check on the children who, like Madison, were waiting between immunotherapy treatments. It felt as if she was avoiding him as much as she could.

He could understand why. After all, he'd been the one to back off on Sunday morning. He hadn't even given her a proper explanation, because he couldn't find the right words and he'd been selfish enough to take the easy option of saying nothing. To back away, just as he always did.

He sighed inwardly. He hadn't been fair to Rosie. He knew he ought to let her go, because he couldn't offer her a future; yet, at the same time, he was drawn to her and to the way that he'd felt as if he were part of a family on Saturday night. The whole thing threw him. He wasn't used to feeling confused and torn like this—torn between doing what he knew was the right thing and doing what he really wanted to do.

Rosie Hobbes was special. Walking away from her might be the stupidest thing he'd ever done.

Yet at the same time he knew she was vulnerable; it wouldn't be fair of him to get involved with her and then walk away when his temporary contract came to an end.

The more he worked with her and saw the calm, kind way she dealt with even the most difficult and frightened of their little patients, the more he wanted her in his life.

Should he follow his heart or his head?

He still didn't have an answer by the end of the morning's clinic, but he needed to talk to her. The least she deserved was for him to apologise for backing off on Sunday and to explain why he'd acted so hurtfully.

'Ros—Nurse Hobbes,' he corrected himself. 'Can I talk to you over lunch?'

She shook her head. 'I'm reading to Penny.'

Of course. It was Monday. How could he have forgotten? 'After work?'

Again, she refused. 'I need to pick up the children.'

'Then during your break, this afternoon,' he said. 'I really think we need to talk.'

'There's absolutely nothing to say. We work together.'

But her gaze had lingered just a little too long on his mouth. He had a feeling that she was remembering that kiss on Saturday and it was confusing her as much as it was confusing him. Or was he deluding himself?

'Please,' he said softly. 'Give me a chance to explain.'

She was silent for so long that he thought she was going to say no. Finally, she nodded. 'All right.'

'Coffee at Tony's?' he suggested, thinking there might be a tiny bit more privacy there than in the hospital canteen.

'There isn't really enough time. I'll meet you in the ward kitchen,' she countered.

He could put up with the vile instant coffee; what bothered him more was that it was usually busy in the ward kitchen. 'I'd rather talk somewhere a little quieter,' he said.

She was implacable. 'That's as quiet as you're going to get.'

'Fair enough.'

To his relief, the kitchen was empty when he got there at the beginning of their afternoon break. He filled the kettle and switched it on, and had just made the coffee when she walked in.

'Thank you,' she said as he handed her the mug.

'No problem, Rosie.' Again, she skewered him with a look for using her first name. He sighed. 'If you would prefer me to call you "Nurse Hobbes", fine—but it's a bit formal for someone who kissed me back on Saturday night.'

'We all make mistakes.'

'Yes, and I made rather more of them than you did, this weekend,' he said wryly. 'Rosie.' This time, to his relief, she didn't correct him. 'I want to spend time with you,' he said. 'You *and* the twins.'

'Which is why you promised them you'd go to the park with us on Sunday, but you called it off at the last minute and didn't even give a reason?' she asked.

He raked a hand through his hair, knowing she was right to be upset with him about it. 'I wanted to go. But the three of you are vulnerable, and I don't want to lead you on.'

'It's not fair to Lexi and Freddie to let you into their lives, only for you to disappear again,' she said. 'Do you even know how long you're going to be in London? You're on a temporary con-tract, after all.'

'It's for a couple of months, but we might be able to extend it. If not, there are other hospitals in London.'

She frowned. 'So now you tell me that you're planning to stay in London?'

He couldn't answer that properly. 'It's possible.'

'Even so, you're a duke and I don't have even a drop of blue blood. I'm a single mum of two, and I'm just about the most unsuitable person you could get involved with.'

'You're kind, you're straight-talking and you're sweet,' he corrected, 'and I don't care about blue blood or difficult pasts.'

'You might not,' she said dryly, 'but your fam-ily might.'

'The one person who might've protested—no, I'll be honest with you,' he corrected himself, '*would* have protested, is dead.'

She looked completely confused.

He sighed. 'I trust you to keep my confidence, the way I'm keeping yours about Michael.'

She flinched, then nodded. 'Of course.'

'I didn't have the greatest time growing up.' It

was the first time he'd really talked about it to anyone, and it made him uncomfortable. Like rubbing on a bruise so deep it hadn't even started colouring his skin yet. 'My father had pretty set views on life. I knew I was supposed to study for some kind of business degree to prepare me for taking over my father's duties on the estate and eventually inheriting the dukedom, and I guess I rebelled by going to university in Rome rather than nearby in Florence. I thought I'd get a bit more freedom there.'

'But you didn't?'

He shrugged. 'At first, I really thought I had. I fell in love with a girl I met in my first week there—Emilia. I thought she loved me, too. She was sweet and kind and clever, and I was so sure my parents would love her as much as I did.' He paused. 'And then I made the mistake of taking her back to Tuscany for the weekend.'

'Your parents didn't like her?'

'My mother did. My father decided that she wasn't good enough for me. So he warned her off.'

Rosie looked shocked. 'And she accepted that?'

'I didn't realise at the time how much he leaned

on her. She must have resisted him at first, but then suddenly there were all these little administrative mistakes that made her life difficult—her finances were late, or her rent showed up as unpaid, even though she'd paid it and had a receipt. Her marks started dropping and her future at the university was under threat. Her part-time employer suddenly changed his mind about her working for him, and she didn't even get an interview for everything else she applied for. I didn't connect it at the time, but my father was behind it all. The longer Emilia dated me, the harder it got for her, until she did what he wanted and broke up with me. Then she left the university,' he said quietly.

'That's awful,' Rosie said.

'I tried very hard to find her—I even used a private investigator—but she went completely to ground. I had a feeling my father was behind her disappearance, so I confronted him about it.' It had been the worst row they'd ever had. The first time Leo had really stood up for himself. His father had taken it extremely badly. 'Let's just say my father epitomised everything I don't stand for. And that's when I realised that he was never going to change. He'd manipulated her and he was always going to try and manipulate me because that was who he was. I could either let him do it, or I could stop trying to please a man who'd never be pleased, no matter what I did. I might have to inherit the dukedom, but I decided I'd do it my way. I left Rome and I applied to read medicine in London—so I'd have a career where I could give back some of my privileges, instead of trying to take more.'

She reached out and took his hand. 'I'm sorry you didn't have the right support when you were younger.'

'Plenty of people have had it much worse than me. I shouldn't complain.'

'What about your mum? Didn't she try to talk your dad round?'

'My father was quite forceful in his views,' he said. 'It was easier for her to agree with him.'

'That's something I don't understand,' she said softly. 'Because I'd never let anyone hurt my children. Including their father. That's why I left Michael, and why I changed the children's names along with mine.'

'You're a strong woman,' he said. 'Not everyone is like that.' His mother probably would've liked to be, but Leo came from a line of old-fashioned men who believed that a woman's place was to shut up and agree with her husband, and a child's place was to ask 'how high?' when his father said 'jump'. And his mother's family was the same. Even the kindest heart could get beaten into submission. And sometimes words left more scars than physical blows. He could understand now why Beatrice hadn't tried to stand up to her husband.

'Not everyone has the support behind them to help,' Rosie said, going straight to the core of things. 'My family was brilliant. They backed me.'

'You're one of the lucky ones,' he said.

'Did you try looking for Emilia again when you came to London?'

'I found her before that,' he said.

The bleakness in Leo's eyes told Rosie this wasn't a story with a happy ending. 'What happened to her?' she asked gently.

'After Emilia left Italy, she did charity work in Africa. While she was out there, she caught a virus.' He looked away. 'She was too far from the medical care she needed. She never made it home.'

Rosie winced. 'That's so sad. Is that why you chose to study medicine?'

'It's one of the reasons, yes,' he said. 'Plus, everyone's equal in medicine. And it means I can give something back.'

Leo Marchetti was a good deal more complicated than she'd thought he was, Rosie realised. Despite all that privileged upbringing, he'd had his heart well and truly broken. Not just because he'd lost the woman he'd fallen in love with, but because his father sounded like a complete control freak. If he'd been so desperate to control Leo that he'd bullied Emilia into leaving, what else had he done? It sounded as if Leo's mother hadn't been able to stand up to her husband, either.

No wonder Leo was wary about families, after such a miserable childhood. No wonder he hadn't wanted any relationship to get serious. But she came with a family: how could it work out between them?

'So where do we go from here?' she asked.

'If I'm honest, I don't know,' he said. 'I understand why you don't want to get involved. I'm not exactly looking for a relationship, either.'

At least he was up front about it. 'The papers all say you're a playboy.'

He grimaced. 'The press will say anything to sell copies. Yes, I've dated a lot in the past, but I don't make promises I can't keep and I don't lie my way into someone's bed. I offer my girl-friends a good time, yes, but I make it clear that it's fun for now and not for always.'

'I have the twins to think of,' she said. 'I can't just have a fling with you because it's not fair to them. And you can't offer me more than a fling, so...' She spread her hands. 'Maybe we should just call it a day. Maybe we can be friends.'

'I don't want to be just your friend,' he said.

'So what do you want?' she asked.

'That's the thing, Rosie,' he said. 'I want you.'

His dark eyes were soulful and full of sincerity. And even though Rosie found it hard to believe anything a man told her—she'd heard too many lies to take things at face value any more—Leo had shown her that he trusted her. He'd told her things that the gossip magazines would no doubt love to know—and he was trusting her not to break the story to the press. So maybe, just maybe, she could trust him.

'My head's telling me I should back away now—that it's going to cause no end of complications if I do what my heart's telling me to do,' he said.

'What's your heart telling you to do?' she asked.

'Something different. To take a risk,' he said. 'I like you and I think you like me.'

His admission made her feel as if all the air had just been sucked out of her lungs. Yes. She did like Leo. She thought she could like him a lot. But seeing him… Would that be a huge mistake? 'So what are you suggesting?' she asked.

'That we see where this takes us.'

'We've already discussed this. I come as a package, Leo. I have two three-year-olds,' she reminded him.

'I appreciate that, and I'm including them in this whole thing. We've already told them that I'm your friend from work. Right now, they don't need to know anything more complicated than that. As far as they're concerned, you're being kind to me because I don't know many people.

And, actually, that's a really good example to set them.'

Rosie thought about it. Maybe this was a way to have it all—to see Leo on more than just a friendship basis, but for the twins to think that he was just her friend.

But what if she got it wrong? What effect would it have on Lexi and Freddie if they got close to him and then he disappeared out of their lives?

On the other hand, she knew it would be good for Freddie to have another male role model in his life, even if it was only for a little while. And the Leo Marchetti she was beginning to know was a decent man. He'd be a good role model.

'No strings,' she said. 'And the children don't get hurt. They come first.'

'Absolutely,' he said.

Excitement fluttered low down in her belly. This was the first time in nearly five years that she'd agreed to date someone. And Leo Marchetti wasn't just someone: he was the most attractive man she'd met in a very long time.

'So what happens now?' she asked. 'I'm a bit rusty when it comes to dating.'

He smiled. 'It's not exactly the thing I'm best

at, either. Which is how come I've got this stupid reputation as a playboy. Even though I'm not one really.' He swallowed hard. 'Since Emilia, I haven't met anyone I've wanted to get close to. Until now. Until *you*.'

Which was honest. And he'd gone a step further with her, admitting that he didn't have a clue where this was going to take them. 'Thank you for being honest,' she said. And she needed to be equally as straight with him: they didn't have a future. How could they, when their worlds were so different? 'Just so it's clear, I'm not looking for a stepfather for Freddie and Lexi.'

'So is this going to make us friends with benefits?' he asked.

'I don't know—but I think we've all been hurt enough. Just as long as we don't expect too much from each other, I guess.'

'We'll play it by ear, then, and muddle through together,' he suggested.

'OK.'

'When are you free this week?' he asked.

'I was going to take the children to the park on Wednesday, on the way home from here. You could come with us, if you like, and then have dinner with us at home afterwards?'

He smiled. 'Thank you. I'd like that very much.'

Rosie wasn't sure if she was doing the right thing or not, but maybe her sister and her parents and her closest friends were right and it was time to try again, put the past behind her. Leo had been damaged, too, and she realised now that he'd backed away on Sunday more from a fear of hurting anyone than from seeing the children as a burden. Maybe a few dates with no strings would do them both good. 'Wednesday, then. And we're both due back in clinic.'

'Indeed. And thank you, Rosie. For giving us a chance.' He leaned forward and kissed her on the cheek. It was the lightest contact, but it made her skin tingle. And she remembered how it had felt when he'd kissed her properly on Saturday.

A new beginning.

Maybe it wouldn't work out.

But they were both adults. They'd make sure that Freddie and Lexi weren't hurt; and they could try to enjoy this thing between them while it lasted.

CHAPTER SIX

ON WEDNESDAY AFTERNOON, Leo collected something he'd stowed in his locker, then waited for Rosie outside the hospital while she collected the twins from the hospital nursery school.

Lexi gave him an accusing look when they stopped in front of him. 'You didn't come to the park with us. You said you would.'

'I know, and I'm sorry I let you down. But your *mamma* says we can go today on the way home,' Leo said.

'Are you coming with us?' Freddie asked, looking faintly suspicious.

'I am, if you don't mind,' Leo said solemnly. He held out the bag he was carrying. 'I thought maybe we could play ball. If you like playing ball?'

'I want to go on the swings,' Lexi said.

'And I want to go on the slide,' Freddie said.

'How about,' Rosie suggested, 'we do all three?'

The twins looked at each other, then at her, and nodded.

As they walked to the park, Leo was surprised and touched that Freddie wanted to hold his hand on the way. It gave him an odd feeling. He couldn't really remember going to a park when he was small, even with his nanny; whereas clearly this was something that Rosie did regularly with her children and they all looked forward to it.

Once they were at the small enclosed play-ground, Leo pushed Lexi on the swings while Rosie pushed Freddie.

This was all very, very domestic and so far out of Leo's experience that it scared him stu-pid. Though he knew that if he backed away from Rosie again, she wouldn't give him another chance. He had to damp down the fear of the un-known and the fear of getting too involved.

They headed for the slide next. It was high, and wide enough for about four people to go down at a time; Leo was slightly surprised that Rosie, who was a bit on the over-protective side where the twins were concerned, was actually letting them go on it.

'Will you slide down with me, Leo?' Freddie asked.

'What's the missing word, Freddie?' Rosie asked quietly.

'Please,' Freddie added swiftly, and Rosie gave him a thumbs-up.

'Sure,' Leo said. He helped the little boy climb up to the top of the slide and sat down next to him on the platform.

'I have to hold your hand or we can't go down,' Freddie informed him.

Leo wasn't sure whether that was Freddie's way of saying that he was a bit scared, or whether it was one of Rosie's rules to keep her children safe on the slide. Either way, he wasn't going to make a fuss about it. 'Sure,' he said, and held Freddie's hand. 'Ready?'

'Ready,' the little boy confirmed.

'After three. One, two, three—go!'

Rosie took her phone out of her bag and snapped a photograph of them on the way down, then smiled at him as they reached the bottom.

The sudden rush of adrenaline through Leo's blood had nothing to do with the slide and everything to do with that smile.

Lexi and Rosie went next, and Leo took a picture of them on his phone.

'You go down with Mummy, next,' Lexi said when they walked over to Leo and Freddie.

What could he do but agree?

At the top, Freddie called, 'Mummy, take a picture!'

'Do you mind?' Rosie asked.

He knew she wouldn't pass it to the press or make life difficult for him. 'Sure.'

Once Rosie had taken the photo and tucked her phone back into the pocket of her jeans, Lexi called, 'You have to hold hands!'

If he refused, then he'd be undermining Rosie's rule for the children—which wouldn't be fair. If he held her hand, he'd be undermining his own resolve not to get too close. Either way, this was going to be tricky.

'Ready?' Rosie asked softly.

'Yes,' he lied.

She took his hand. His skin tingled where it touched hers and he suddenly really wanted to kiss her, but he managed to hold himself in check. That was absolutely not going to happen in front of the children.

Sliding down towards the children, seeing them clap their hands with glee, made something around the region of his heart feel as if it had just cracked. And then going down the slide again with Lexi, and finally the four of them together, all holding hands and whooping at the same time… It was something he'd never done before. Something that felt really, really good.

They played ball and had another last go on the swings before Rosie called a halt. 'Time for tea,' she said.

'We're having macanoni, 'cause it's Wednesday,' Freddie told him seriously as Rosie unlocked her front door.

Leo hid a smile at the little boy's charming mispronunciation. 'I love macaroni,' he said.

'Good, because I feel a bit bad cooking pasta for an Italian,' Rosie said.

Leo laughed. 'Macaroni cheese isn't actually Italian. It was invented in England.'

'Seriously?'

'Seriously—obviously there have been pasta and cheese dishes in Italy for centuries,' he said, 'and some were even recorded in a fourteenth-century Italian cookbook called *Liber de*

Coquina. There's a version in an English cookery book around the same kind of date, but the first modern recipe for macaroni cheese is actually in an English book from the middle of the eighteenth century.'

Rosie looked even more surprised. 'How do you know this? Did you study cookery or something before you studied medicine?'

'I found out in the general knowledge round at a pub quiz,' he admitted. 'Anyway, I really don't care who invented it. I like it.' He paused. 'Anything I can do to help?'

'Sure. You can help lay the table with Freddie and Lexi, and help them with the drinks,' she said. 'And if you want some wine, there's a bottle in the rack.'

'I'll have whatever you're having,' he said.

She smiled, and his heart felt as if it had done a backflip. 'I like red or white, so pick what you prefer. Oh, and we have strawberries for pudding.'

While the macaroni cheese—which she'd clearly made the previous night—was heating through in the oven, Rosie started chopping salad, and he helped the twins lay the table and put beakers out for water.

'Mummy says we're not big enough to carry a jug yet,' Lexi confided, looking slightly forlorn.

'You will be, soon,' he said, and filled the jug with water before taking it to the table and opening a bottle of red wine for himself and Rosie.

He chatted to the twins while Rosie finished up in the kitchen, enjoying the way they opened up to him and told him all about their day, what they'd drawn and sung and glued. And it somehow felt natural to let them curl up each side of him on the sofa and teach him one of their nursery songs.

Rosie lingered in the doorway, watching Leo with her two very earnest children. Of course he was good with kids; it was his day job, after all. But she liked the way he behaved with them, persuading them to take turns and giving shy Freddie that little bit of extra encouragement so his confidence started to grow to match his sister's.

Was Leo Marchetti the one who could change her life for the better?

Or would he back away again when he realised

that treating children in a hospital was very different from living with them every day?

At least they'd agreed that he wouldn't let the children get too attached to him: that as far as the twins were concerned Leo was simply her colleague and a friend, and not a potential replacement father.

She brought in the dish of macaroni cheese and served up, encouraging the twins to add salad to their plates.

'This is very nice. Thank you,' Leo said after his first forkful.

Was he just being polite? Rosie wondered. This was a far cry from his normal life. Although she was a reasonable cook, she didn't kid herself that she made anything exceptional. This was all just ordinary stuff. Very domestic. A world away from how the Duke of Calvanera lived.

Once they'd finished their pasta and demolished a large bowl of strawberries between them, Rosie announced that it was time for bath and bed.

'But we want to stay up with Leo!' Lexi protested.

'Bath and bed now,' Rosie said firmly. 'Otherwise you'll be too tired to do anything at nursery school tomorrow morning. And I happen to know you're doing splatter painting tomorrow.'

'Yay! My favourite,' Freddie said. 'Lexi, we have to have our bath now.'

'I'll do the washing up,' Leo offered.

Rosie shook her head. 'It's fine. I understand if you need to get on.'

'No. You cooked. Washing up is the least I can do,' Leo said.

'Will you read us another bedtime story?' Lexi asked.

'Please?' Freddie added.

'That's up to your mum,' Leo said.

How could she refuse? 'If you don't mind, Leo, that would be lovely.'

He came upstairs when she'd got the twins bathed and in their pyjamas. 'So what story would you like tonight?'

'The dinosaur story, please!' they chorused.

Rosie leaned against the door jamb and watched him read to the children. He seemed to be enjoying himself, and the children enjoyed it enough to cajole him into reading a second story to them.

'Time to say goodnight,' she said gently when

he'd finished, knowing that they could badger him into half a dozen more stories.

Lexi held her arms up towards him. 'Kiss goodnight,' she said sleepily.

'Me, too,' Freddie said, doing the same.

Leo glanced at Rosie for permission. Part of her felt she ought to say no—she didn't want Leo getting close to the children and then leaving. Yet how could she deprive them of that warmth—a simple, sweet kiss goodnight? She gave a tiny nod.

'Goodnight. Sleep tight,' he whispered, kissing each of them on the forehead in turn, and being hugged tightly by both twins.

'Thank you,' she said quietly when they were downstairs again. 'I appreciate you being kind to them.'

'They're lovely children,' Leo said.

Was that a hint of wistfulness she saw in his face? she wondered.

'And I enjoyed this evening. I can't remember the last time I went down a slide.'

Definitely wistfulness, Rosie thought. Leo clearly hadn't had much of a chance to visit a playground when he was young. Poor little rich boy, probably having everything his parents could buy him and yet not having a normal childhood where he was free to run and laugh and play.

'I'm glad you came with us.' She paused. 'Would you like another glass of wine?'

He shook his head. 'I left my car at the hospital.'

Which was his cue to leave. And probably the best thing, she thought.

'But I'd like to stay for a little longer, if that's OK with you,' he said.

He rested his palm against her cheek, and her mouth went dry.

It went drier still when he rubbed the pad of his thumb against her lower lip.

And then he bent his head and brushed his mouth against hers. What else could she do but slide her hands round his neck and lean against him, letting him deepen the kiss?

She was dizzy by the time he broke the kiss.

'My beautiful Rosie,' he whispered. 'Right now I just want to hold you.'

Unable to form any kind of coherent sentence, she simply nodded.

She hadn't expected him to scoop her up and

carry her to the sofa, and it made her knees go weak. 'That's...' All the rest of the words went out of her head when he sat down and settled her on his lap.

'A bit caveman-like,' he finished wryly. 'But you're irresistible. You remind me of Titian's *Flora.*'

'Flora?'

He took his phone from his pocket, looked up the portrait on the Internet and handed the phone to her. 'Obviously your hair's shorter—but you're beautiful, like her.'

All curves, Rosie thought as she looked at the portrait. Michael had liked her curves until she was pregnant; then he'd considered her to be fat and unattractive.

She pushed the thought away and handed the phone back to Leo. 'Thank you for the compliment. Sorry. I don't know a lot about art.'

'I spent a lot of time in the Uffizi in my teens,' he said. 'This was always one of my favourites.' He stole another kiss. 'Tell me about your teens.'

'There isn't really that much to tell. I spent my time with my sister and friends, doing the kind of things teenage girls do,' she said. 'Trying out different make-up, doing each other's hair, talking and listening to music.' She smiled. 'And films. Monday night was cheap night when I was a student nurse, so a group of us used to go out every Monday when we weren't on placement or doing a late shift.'

'Any particular favourites?' he asked.

'We'd see anything and everything,' she said. 'Freddie and Lexi like the cinema, too. I try to take them to see all the animated films, because they're so magical on a big screen. One or other of them always needs the loo halfway through, but they love going to see a film.'

Again, he looked wistful. Clearly his parents hadn't done that sort of thing with him when he was young. 'Maybe we could do something like that at the weekend.'

'Maybe,' she said. 'So your teens were spent mooching about museums?'

'And studying. And trying to wriggle out of deadly dull functions.'

Where his father had shown him off as the heir? She sensed it was a sore spot, but she didn't know what to say. The only thing she could think of to do was to kiss him. Judging by how dark his eyes were when she finally broke the kiss, it had been the right thing to do.

She stayed curled on his lap with her arms round him, just chatting idly. Finally, he stole a last kiss. 'I'd better let you get some sleep.'

'Are you OK to get back to your car from here?'

He smiled. 'Yes, but thanks for asking.'

She had the strongest feeling that people didn't tend to try to look after Leo Marchetti very much. Maybe it was because he was so capable and efficient at work; or maybe it was because everyone assumed that the Duke's personal staff kept his life completely in order. But did anyone really see the man behind the doctor and the dukedom? 'I'll see you at work tomorrow, then.'

'Yes. Goodnight.'

Rosie was still smiling when she'd finished brushing her teeth and was curled up in bed. Just spending time with Leo had felt so good. Her children liked him, too. So did she dare to keep dreaming that this might actually work out?

On Thursday, Leo was working in clinic while Rosie was working on the ward, but he caught up with her at lunchtime.

'Had a good morning?' he asked.

'Yes and no.' She sighed. 'I was looking after young Ryan today.'

'How's he doing?'

'He's showing small signs of improvement, but he's still unconscious.' She bit her lip. 'It's really tough on his parents.'

'Do you think he's going to recover?' Leo asked.

'I really don't know. In some respects, it's kind of early days; in others, it…' She shook her head and grimaced. 'And then there's Penny.'

The young patient who was a favourite with everyone who met her. 'She's on the transplant list now?'

'Yes. And now it's a waiting game.' Rosie stared into her coffee. 'They're both so young. And, despite all the advances in medicine and the different treatments, are we really going to make the right difference to either of them?'

'Yes. Years ago, they wouldn't even have come this far,' Leo reminded her. 'But you're right. It's hard on the parents.'

'I was just thinking. If the worst happens—and I really hope it doesn't, for his family's sake—

then it would be good if Ryan turned out to be a match for Penny,' Rosie said softly.

'So at least one of them would be saved?'

She nodded, and he reached across the table to squeeze her hand briefly.

'Sometimes this job is tough,' he said.

'You're telling me.' She blew out a breath. 'Sometimes I look at Penny and Ryan and Simon, and it makes me want to run down to the hospital nursery school so I can hug Freddie and Lexi really, really tightly.'

'Of course it does. You're a mum, so you have a pretty good idea of what your patients' parents are feeling.'

'I just wish I had a magic wand.'

'Me, too,' he agreed softly. 'But we're doing the best we can.' Even if it sometimes felt as though it wasn't enough.

On Friday night, Leo texted Rosie.

Do you want to go to the cinema tomorrow? Have looked at schedules.

Nothing really suitable, was the reply.

Was she backing away from him?
His phone beeped again.

How about the aquarium?

Fine. Meet you when and where?

Tube station at ten? she suggested.

I'll be there.

She was already there when he walked to meet her. The twins jumped about in excitement when he walked up to them, and hugged him round his knees—something he hadn't expected, and another little shard of ice around his heart melted.

'We're going to see the sharks!' Freddie said.

'And the starfishies,' Lexi added. 'I love starfishies.'

Clearly this was something they were really looking forward to. It was another thing way outside his experience, but Leo found himself thoroughly enjoying the visit, and the twins' excitement was definitely infectious. He lifted one or the other up every so often so they could have a closer look at the occupants of a tank; and he noticed that Rosie got them to count the fish and name colours and shapes.

'How many arms does your starfish have?' he asked Lexi.

She counted them, then beamed at him. 'Five!'

'Well done.' He smiled back at her.

There was a play area in the central hall where the youngest children could do colouring and older ones could answer quizzes. On impulse, when Lexi and Freddie sat down, he crouched beside them. 'Shall I draw something for you to colour?'

'Yes, please!' they chorused.

'A shark for you, Lexi, and a starfish for you, Freddie?' he asked, teasing them.

'No, that's silly—it's the other way round!' Lexi said.

Freddie just clapped his hands with glee as he watched Leo draw.

He glanced up at Rosie. Were those tears he saw in her eyes? But why? What had he done wrong?

Once they'd finished laboriously colouring in the shapes, they looked at Rosie. 'Can you write our names, please, Mummy?' Lexi asked.

'Sure. Can you spell them for me?' Rosie asked. Leo watched as both children looked very earnest and spelled out their names phonetically; Rosie wrote down what they said.

'Thank you, Mummy,' Freddie said, then turned to Leo and gave him the shark picture. 'This is for you.'

'So's this,' Lexi added, not to be outdone and thrusting her starfish picture at him.

'Thank you, both of you,' Leo said. 'I'll put the pictures up when I get home.'

'On your fridge, like Mummy does?' Lexi wanted to know.

'Absolutely like Mummy does,' he said with a smile.

When they walked through the shark tunnel, the twins were both shrieking with joy and pointing out the sharks swimming overhead. Rosie was smiling, but she took their hands and crouched down beside them for a moment. 'I know you're excited, but you'll scare the sharks if you keep screaming. Can we pretend to be mice?'

'But mice don't live in the sea,' Freddie said. 'They live in houses.'

'You could be a new species,' Leo said. 'Sea mice.'

The twins thought about it, then nodded and were much quieter—still pointing out the sharks but careful to whisper.

Rosie caught Leo's eye. 'Thank you,' she mouthed.

Once they were through the tunnel and Rosie had bought a new storybook about Sammy the Shy Shark, they headed out to the South Bank. They all enjoyed hot dogs from one of the street food vendors, then sat down on a bench to eat *churros* with chocolate sauce while they watched some of the street entertainers, a juggler and a woman making balloon dogs. Both children ended up with their faces covered with chocolate, and Leo made the mistake of buying them each a balloon dog before Rosie had wiped their hands and faces clear—they insisted on kissing him thank you, smearing his cheeks with chocolate.

Rosie laughed and took a photograph of them all posing with chocolaty faces before giving him a wipe from her handbag and cleaning the twins up.

By the time they were back at Rosie's, the children were worn out. They managed half a sandwich before they nearly fell asleep at the table.

'No bath tonight, I think,' she said with a smile. 'Straight to bed with a story.'

Leo helped her get the children into their pyjamas and tucked them in; again, the domestic nature and the closeness made him feel as if something was cracking around his heart.

'I didn't think about dinner tonight. The best I can offer is a takeaway,' she said.

'Which would be lovely. And I'll pay, because you fed me on Wednesday,' he said.

They shared a Chinese meal, then curled up on the sofa. 'I meant to ask you earlier,' he said. 'What did I do to upset you?'

'Upset me?' She looked confused.

'In the aquarium. You looked as if you were blinking back tears.'

'Ah. That.' Her face cleared. 'You drew them a picture of their favourite sea creatures so they could colour them in.'

She didn't say it, but he had the strongest feeling that Michael had never done anything like that. 'I didn't mean to make you cry.'

'They were happy tears,' she said softly.

'Even so, I can still kiss you better.' And how right it felt, to hold her close and kiss her until they were both dizzy.

Leo was beginning to think that this might be what he actually wanted his life to be like—a job he adored at the hospital, and the warmth and domesticity of Rosie and the twins. He just needed to find a way to square it with his duties in Tuscany. Though he knew it was way too early to be thinking about that. For now, he'd just enjoy spending time with her.

At the end of the evening, he kissed her goodnight. 'See you at work on Monday.'

'See you Monday,' she agreed. 'And thank you for today. I had a fabulous time and so did the twins.'

'Me, too,' he said.

'Oh, before I forget.' She rummaged in her handbag and brought out a tiny paper bag with the logo of the aquarium on it.

'What's this?' he asked.

'Just a little something.'

He opened the bag to find two magnets: one shaped like a shark and one like a pink starfish.

'You told the twins you were going to put their pictures on your fridge. I'm guessing that you might be a bit short on magnets,' she explained.

'I am,' he agreed. His flat was pristine, like a show house, with no little decorative touches whatsoever. The magnets and the pictures might just be the first step to turning it into a home. 'Thank you.' He kissed her again, more lingeringly this time. 'Monday.'

'Monday,' she said.

And for the first time in a very long time, Monday morning felt like a promise.

CHAPTER SEVEN

'ARE YOU BUSY at the weekend?' Leo asked Rosie on Monday evening.

'Why?'

He stole a kiss. 'It's rude to answer a question with a question.'

'I don't have anything planned,' she said.

'Good.' He paused. 'Do the children have passports?'

'Yes, though they haven't actually been abroad. Why?'

'I was just wondering—would you like to come to Tuscany for the weekend?'

She blinked. 'Tuscany? Are you...' It was suddenly hard to breathe. 'Leo, are you asking me to meet your family?'

'Yes and no,' Leo hedged.

'Which doesn't exactly tell me anything,' she pointed out.

'There aren't any strings. I need to be in Tuscany for the weekend, and I thought you and the children might like to enjoy a bit of summer sun. Plus, I've been telling Lexi that the best ice cream ever comes from Italy, and it's about time I proved it.'

'So would we be staying at your family home?'

'The Palazzo di Calvanera. Yes.' He smiled at her. 'Mamma's a little frail. Although I speak to her every day, and I know her companion will tell me if she's in the slightest bit worried about my mother's health, I like to keep an eye on her myself as well. Going to see her at the weekend will put my mind at rest.'

Of course Leo would be a dutiful son.

But Rosie also remembered what he'd told her about Emilia, the girl he'd fallen in love with at university. The girl his family hadn't considered good enough for him. Would Leo's mother decide that, as a single mum of two, Rosie was also completely the wrong sort of person for her son?

'Maybe your mother would prefer you to visit on your own,' she suggested warily.

'I'm sure she'd enjoy meeting you and the children.'

How could she explain her worries? That this

was suddenly sounding really serious—as if he was starting to expect things of their relationship? Things that she might not be able to deliver? 'You and me… It's still very early days,' she said.

'True.' He drew her hand up to his mouth and kissed the backs of her fingers.

'I don't want to give your mother the wrong impression.'

'There's no pressure,' he reassured her. 'I just thought you might like to see the *palazzo*. It has an amazing rose garden. And a lake. The children will love running around the place.'

A lake. Which might not be fenced off. Which would be dangerous for the children. She pushed the thoughts away. She could run faster than they could, and she could swim. There was a more immediate danger than the one she was imagining. 'Meeting your mother—does that mean you expect to meet my family?'

'I've already met the twins,' he pointed out.

'That isn't what I mean, and you know it. This thing between us… We agreed we'd take things slowly and see what happened.'

'Which is exactly what we're doing.'

What, when he was asking them to visit his family home and to meet his mother?

Her doubts must have shown on her face, because he said again, 'Rosie, there's no pressure. Tuscany will just be a little break for us, that's all. A chance to have some fun. And I can show Freddie the suits of armour and Lexi all the portraits of the Duchesses.'

He wasn't playing fair. He knew she'd find it hard to say no where her children were concerned. 'Supposing your mother doesn't like me?'

'My mother,' he said softly, 'will like you very much. You're honest, you're open and you're caring. And she's not bothered about blue blood.'

But his father had been very bothered indeed.

Again, her feelings must have shown on her face, because he added, 'My father would have thought you way too uppity. You wouldn't have liked him very much, either. But Mamma's different. She doesn't share his views. You'll like each other.'

'I don't know,' she said.

'If you're worried about the travelling, I'm using a friend's plane. There won't be lots of queuing at the airport or anything.'

She blinked. 'Hang on. You're using a private plane?'

'It's not as fancy as it sounds. It's quite small,' Leo said.

'My friends own *cars*, not planes.' She couldn't quite get her head round this. 'Leo, I think your world is very, very different from mine.'

'Not at heart, it isn't. And actually I was going to ask you a favour over the weekend.'

'So there are strings attached?'

'No. Of course not.' He frowned. 'You can say no. But part of my duties... The main reason I'm going back is because there's a charity ball in aid of a clinic I support, and I need to be there.'

'What kind of clinic?'

'Paediatric medicine. For children whose families can't afford to pay for treatment,' he explained.

She frowned. 'So healthcare in Italy isn't like it is in England?'

'It's actually very similar, a mix of public and private healthcare,' he said. 'Family doctors are paid for by the Ministry of Health, like they are here in England, and emergency care and surgery are both free. You pay some money towards medication, depending on your income; and if your family doctor refers you to a specialist or for diagnostic tests, you only have to pay a little bit towards it. But waiting times can be quite long, so there are private hospitals where you can pay a bit more money to see the specialist or have treatment a bit sooner.'

'And that's what this clinic is? A private hospital, except patients don't pay?'

He nodded. 'I also work there when I'm in Italy.'

He'd said that he had an interest in philanthropic medicine. Obviously supporting this clinic was part of that, Rosie thought.

'So I was wondering if you might accompany me to the ball.'

'What about the children?' Rosie asked. They could hardly go to a glitzy ball. Apart from the fact that they were too young to attend in the first place, the ball probably wouldn't start until way past their bedtime.

'I can arrange a babysitter for them,' he said.

'No.'

He frowned. 'What do you mean, no?'

'Leo, do you really expect me to leave my children in a strange place with someone I don't know?'

'It's my home, and I know the babysitter,' he pointed out. 'I think I already told you that my mother has a companion, Violetta. Her daughter Lisetta lives nearby and I'm sure she'd be very happy to babysit.'

So he hadn't even asked the babysitter yet? Then again, that was fair—he hadn't known if Rosie would say yes or no to his invitation. Even so, the whole idea freaked her. 'Leo, the point is that *I* don't know her,' she countered. 'Yes, I know it's your home, but do you seriously think I'd be happy to leave my children in a country where they don't speak the language—where *I* don't speak the language, for that matter—with someone they don't know and I don't know?' She took a deep breath. 'Look, I know I'm overprotective, but no mother on earth would agree to anything like that.'

He looked at her. 'But *I* know Lisetta. I've known her for years. Isn't that good enough?'

'How can you not see that it isn't?' Rosie asked.

Leo thought about it. Part of him thought that Rosie was being unreasonable; it wasn't as if he was asking her to leave the children with someone who was a complete stranger. He'd known Lisetta since she was small, and he knew she was kind and she was good with children. Then again, a year ago, Rosie's husband's associate had threatened to hurt the children. Of course she'd be more protective than the average parent.

'I've known Lisetta for years and I trust her,' he said. 'Of course I understand that you're worried. It's natural. But I trust Lisetta, and I hope you know me well enough to realise that I'd be careful with your children and I wouldn't expect you to leave them with just anybody. I also have a security team at the *palazzo*, so no stranger will ever get anywhere near the children. They'll be perfectly safe. I guarantee that.'

She blew out a breath. 'OK. Let's put it another way. Your mum's not in the best of health. Would you bring her over to London and then

leave her on her own for the evening with someone she didn't know—someone who didn't speak
the same language as her—while you went out
partying?'

'It isn't partying. It's a charity ball and attend-
ing it is part of my duties to the clinic—to the estate, actually, because some of the funds for the
clinic come from the estate. Anyway, my mother
speaks good English, and so does Lisetta. There
won't be a language barrier for the children.'

Rosie put her hands over her face and groaned
in apparent frustration. 'You're really not listening to me. Would you leave your mother with
someone she didn't know and you didn't know,
either—say, my neighbour?'

'If you vouched for your neighbour, then yes.
Your word is good enough for me.'

'And I guess in that situation your mother could
call you if there was a problem. But it's not the
same thing for the children. The twins won't be
able to call me if they're worried. They're only
three.' She shook her head. 'It's lovely of you to
ask me, Leo, but I really can't leave them with a
stranger, even though she's somebody you know.
I just can't do it.'

'What if,' Leo said, 'we took a babysitter with us—someone you know?'

'How do you mean?'

'The twins talk a lot about Nina from the nursery school. I'd be happy to pay her to come with us for the weekend, if she's free. Obviously I'll organise things so she flies with us and she'll stay with us at the *palazzo*. Would that make you able to come to the ball with me?'

'I…' She looked torn.

'Rosie. Of course the children come first. Always,' he emphasised. 'But you also need some time for you. You're their mum, yes, and that's important; but that's not all of who you are. You're also a person in your own right. Come and have some fun with me. Just for a few hours. Dinner, a little dancing. I promise you'll be home by midnight.'

'I don't speak any Italian.'

That was a much easier problem to overcome. 'I can teach you a couple of phrases and translate for you if you need me to, and anyway, a lot of people at the ball will speak English.'

She bit her lip. 'Leo, I'm sorry, but this is a big deal. I really need to think about it.'

At least it wasn't a flat no. 'All right.' He paused. 'If you do say yes, then I'd like to buy you a dress for the occasion.'

'I'm perfectly capable of buying my own…' Her voice tailed off as she clearly realised what the ball entailed. 'It's a formal ball. That means black tie and haute couture, doesn't it?'

'White tie,' he said.

'Which is even more posh!'

'It's not that different. A white bow tie and waistcoat instead of a black bow tie.'

'But it's a proper tailcoat, not a dinner jacket.'

'Yes.'

She grimaced. 'If I go—and I do mean *if*—then maybe I can hire a dress from one of those agencies that specialise in posh clothes.'

'Or alternatively you could let me buy you a dress. Not because I'm trying to control you,' he said carefully—he definitely wasn't walking in his father's shoes, 'but because you'd be doing me a huge favour and you shouldn't be out of pocket for being kind.'

'I'll think about it.' She took a deep breath. 'You said about going this weekend. That's not when the ball is, though, is it?'

'Um, actually—yes.'

She blinked. 'That's not a lot of notice, Leo.'

'I know.' He stole a kiss. 'Obviously I've known about the ball for a while. But when I originally arranged to attend it I didn't know I was going to work in London, or that I was going to meet you.'

She bit her lip. 'I'm really not sure about this.'

'Talk it over with someone you trust,' he said. 'If you decide to come with me, then maybe we can go shopping for a dress on Thursday night. Babysitter permitting, of course.'

'All right.'

'Tell me your decision on Wednesday,' he said. 'Will that give you enough time to think about it?'

'I guess so.' Though she didn't sound sure. Clearly he'd pushed her too far, too fast.

'No strings,' he said again. 'If you say no, I won't be offended. But I'd like to spend some time with you and the children.'

That evening, after Leo had gone, Rosie texted her sister.

Need some advice. Are you free tomorrow night?

Daisy rang her straight away. 'I can talk now.'

Oh, help. That didn't give her any time to think about what she was going to say. 'Uh-huh.'

'Rosie? What's wrong?'

'Not wrong, exactly.' She sighed. 'I've been, um, seeing someone.'

'Seriously? That's great! So come on—tell me everything. What's his name, how did you meet him, what's he like?'

She should've known that her sister would give her a barrage of questions. She answered them in order. 'Leo, at work, and he's nice.'

'So why do you need advice?'

This was complicated. 'Daze—I need this to be confidential, OK?'

'Now you're worrying me. Please tell me you haven't met another Michael.'

'He's about as opposite from Michael as you can get,' Rosie reassured her.

'So what's the problem?'

'He's working here on a temporary contract. He's from Italy. And he wants the children and me to go to Italy with him at the weekend.'

'This weekend? To meet his family?'

'Yes. And to go to a charity ball.'

'A charity ball.' Daisy sounded concerned. 'That's a bit flashy. Actually, Ro, that sounds like Michael.'

'It's not quite the same. The ball's in aid of a paediatric clinic that Leo supports. They treat children from families who can't afford to pay,' Rosie explained.

'Whereas Michael would've been all about the glitz and the glamour and it wouldn't actually matter what the charity was,' Daisy said dryly. 'OK.'

'I, um, neglected to tell you that he's also a duke.'

'A duke? What? So how come he's a doctor if he's a duke?'

'It's complicated. But he's a good man, Daze. The children like him.'

'Hang on. He's met the children, and you hardly know him?' Daisy sounded even more shocked.

Rosie squirmed. 'I didn't behave very well. He kept asking me out and he wouldn't take no for an answer. I said yes and met him with the twins. I, um, assumed he'd take one look at the twins and bolt. But he was good with them, Daze. Really sweet.'

'I'm trying to work this out. You've only known him a little while?'

'A couple of weeks,' Rosie confirmed.

'I'm still trying to get my head round the fact that you've let him anywhere near the children.'

'Because he'd need ten people to vouch for him in writing, and sign it in blood?' Rosie asked wryly. 'I'm not that bad, Daze.'

Her sister's silence said otherwise.

Rosie sighed. 'They think he's Mummy's friend who just started at the hospital and doesn't know many people yet, so they're being kind and being his new friends, too.'

'And Freddie actually talks to him?'

'Freddie's really come out of his shell with him,' Rosie said. 'Lexi likes him, too.' She bit her lip. 'But it's going too far, too fast.'

'Maybe not. If Freddie's talking to him that tells me the guy has to be something special,' Daisy said. 'So what's the problem with Italy and the ball? Apart from the fact that it sounds as if he only just asked you and that's not a lot of notice, I mean.'

'He wants someone he knows to look after the twins.'

'Someone you don't know. And you said no.' Daisy paused. 'Does he know about Michael and that debt-collector?'

'Yes. I'm not being overprotective of the children, am I?'

'You're pretty much a helicopter mum,' Daisy said, 'but in the circumstances it's understandable.'

'Then he suggested we could ask Nina from the nursery school to go with us, to look after the children—he's going to pay her if she can do it.' Rosie took a deep breath. 'He said he thinks we all need a bit of fun.'

'He's got a very good point,' Daisy said. 'It's way past time you had some fun in your life. You've been a single parent for a year; and Michael left you to do everything for the twins, so you were practically a single parent before that, too. The only thing you've gone to without them was your ward's Christmas meal last year, and I had to nag you into that. Go and enjoy it, Ro.'

'Really?'

'Really,' Daisy said. 'What are you going to wear?'

'It's a posh do. He, um, offered to buy me a dress.' There had been a time when she'd had several suitable dresses. She'd sold them all to help pay off the debts Michael had left her with. Nowadays, she lived in either her nurse's uniform or casual clothes, neither of which would be remotely suitable. 'That's not because he's being flashy, but because he says I shouldn't be out of pocket for doing him a favour.'

'Actually, he sounds really thoughtful. *Nice*,' Daisy said. 'When are you going shopping?'

'If I say yes, it'll be Thursday night.' She paused. 'Daze, I know it's short notice, but could you—?'

'Of course I'll babysit,' Daisy interrupted. 'And then I get to meet him when you bring him home. If I think he's a Michael in disguise, I'll tell you and you can back out. If he's not, then you can go to Italy and have some fun with him. When's the last time you went out dancing?'

'Before the twins were born,' Rosie admitted.

'So that's well over three years. Go,' Daisy said. 'And if Nina can't come with you at the weekend, I will.'

'Daze, that's…' Rosie felt her eyes film with tears.

'That's what sisters are for. You'd do it for me if I was in your shoes,' Daisy said.

'Thank you.'

'So I'll pick the children up from the nursery school at five on Thursday.'

Daisy was on the very short list of people who were authorised to pick the twins up in Rosie's absence; in accordance with the nursery school rules, Rosie had supplied photographs and code words, so she knew that it wouldn't be a problem.

'Thanks, Daze. I owe you one.'

'Just make sure you've got pizza, dough balls and strawberries in your fridge on Thursday, and we're quits,' her sister said, laughing. 'I love you, Ro. And it'll be so nice to see you having a bit of fun, for once.'

It turned out that Nina was free at the weekend and was more than happy to come to Italy with them. So on Thursday evening Rosie went shopping with Leo.

She stared at him in dismay as they reached

the doors of a very posh department store. 'Leo, this place is really pricey.'

He shrugged. 'I hear their dresses are nice.'

'But—'

'But nothing,' he said gently. 'You need a dress for the ball.'

'It makes me feel a bit like Cinderella,' she muttered.

'Firstly,' he said, 'I'm not Prince Charming. Secondly, you're a first-class nurse, not a kid whose family treats her badly and turns her into a skivvy. And, thirdly, is it so bad to enjoy a little bit of glitz and glamour just for one evening?'

When the price was as high as she'd paid with Michael, yes.

'I said there were no strings,' he said. 'And I meant it.'

And she was behaving like a whiny, attention-seeking brat. He was trying to do something nice for her, and she was practically throwing it back in his face.

'Thank you,' she said, determined to make the effort so he felt appreciated.

Once she'd pushed Michael to the back of her

mind, she actually found herself enjoying the evening, trying on different dresses.

'Might I make a suggestion?' the assistant asked.

'Sure,' Rosie said.

'With your hair, this one will look stunning,' the assistant said, and brought out a turquoise floor-length chiffon gown. The dress had a sweetheart neckline, and white lace and sparkling crystals adorned the straps.

'Your hair and the dress are the opposites on the colour wheel,' the assistant said. 'And I know the perfect shoes for this, too. What size are you?'

'Five and a half,' Rosie said. 'Standard width.'

'Wonderful. Leave this to me.'

By the time Rosie had changed into the dress, the assistant had brought over a pair of copper-coloured strappy high heels. They fitted perfectly.

'Would you like to show your boyfriend?' the assistant asked.

Leo wasn't exactly her boyfriend... 'OK,' she said.

The look on his face when she walked out of the changing room told her everything. And warmth spread through her when he opened his mouth and no words came out. Could she really make this clever, gorgeous man speechless?

'You look amazing,' he said finally. 'Well, you look amazing in jeans as well. But that dress is perfect.'

'Thank you.'

'But you need an evening bag as well.'

'Why?' she asked.

'For your phone,' he said. 'Because I presume you're going to call Nina on the hour to check on the twins.'

She winced; she'd sent Daisy three texts already this evening. 'Am I being overprotective?'

'A little,' he said. 'But I understand why.'

'Thank you. And I do appreciate...' She gestured to the dress.

'My pleasure. You look amazing,' Leo said again.

'Thank you. But I feel guilty about you spending so much money on me.'

'You're doing me a favour,' he reminded her. 'As I said, you shouldn't be out of pocket for that.'

Once she'd changed back into her everyday clothes, the assistant had found the perfect sequin bag to match the shoes and Leo had paid for her outfit, he took the bags, slid his free arm round her shoulders and shepherded her out of the shop. 'Dinner?' he asked. 'And I'm pretty sure you texted your sister at least twice to check on the twins, so if there was a problem we'd have been on our way back to yours an hour ago.'

'Busted,' she admitted. 'And I sent her a picture of me in the dress.'

'And she approved?'

'Very much so.' She felt the colour flicker into her face. 'She said not to rush back.'

'Dinner, then,' he said.

He found a small restaurant, and she smiled as she glanced through the menu. 'This would definitely be too fancy for the twins. I can't remember the last time I ate out at a restaurant where I didn't check the menu out beforehand to make sure it was child-friendly.'

'Enjoy,' he said. 'And this is my treat. No arguments.'

'Thank you,' she said.

The food was amazing: crab with avocado and grapefruit, followed by pan-fried halibut on a bed of seaweed with morels and Jersey royals. She had just enough room left afterwards to share a passion fruit *crème brûlée* with him; and it was oddly intimate, sharing a dessert so that every so often their fingers brushed together.

This felt like a proper date.

The first she'd been on for years and years.

It made her feel unexpectedly shy.

'Everything OK?' he asked.

She nodded. 'You and me, on our own.'

'I enjoy being with the children,' he said. 'But it's also nice to be with you on our own, too.'

She liked the fact that he was still putting the twins first—the way their own father hadn't.

And holding hands with him across the table while they had coffee and *petits fours* felt incredibly romantic. He clearly felt the same, because he held her hand all the way home.

She paused on the doorstep. 'Given that I'll be meeting your family this weekend, would you like to meet my sister this evening?' Or was this rushing things too much?

'I'd love to meet her,' he said.

'Come in,' she said, and opened the front door.

The woman who emerged from the living room looked very like Rosie, Leo thought, with the same copper-coloured hair and bright blue eyes. Rosie didn't even need to introduce them because it was so obvious that the other woman was her sister.

'Ro, the twins are both asleep—and, no, you don't have to rush up to check on them, because you know I won't let anything happen to them.' She smiled at him. 'I'm Daisy, Rosie's big sister. You must be Leo.'

Direct and to the point. He liked that. He shook her hand. 'I'm very pleased to meet you.'

'I hear you're taking my sister to Italy for the weekend.'

'No strings, no pressure, and the children come first,' he said immediately.

'I'm glad to hear it.' She smiled again. 'Come and help me make coffee while my little sister completely ignores what I said and rushes upstairs to check on her babies. And considering she's had several text updates from me...'

'Sorry,' Rosie mouthed, and fled upstairs.

'What you're doing for her—it's nice,' Daisy said.

'But she's already been hurt by a man who swept her off her feet, offered her the good life and let her down. I think the English saying is "handsome is as handsome does",' Leo said.

Daisy nodded. 'I realise you don't plan to do that to her, or you wouldn't even be discussing it with me.'

'Life is complicated,' Leo said. 'And sometimes I think you need to grab happiness with both hands, even if you find it in a place where you didn't expect it.'

'True,' Daisy said.

'I'll be careful with them,' Leo said softly. 'All of them.'

'Good.' Daisy took the coffee from the fridge. 'That's all I ask.'

'And it's nice that she has family to look out for her.'

'You don't?'

He coughed. 'I imagine that Rosie's already told you who I am and you've checked me out online.'

'Isn't that what you'd do if you had a little sister?' Daisy countered.

'Absolutely.'

'The gossip columns say you stop at three dates,' Daisy said.

That stupid reputation. He loathed it. 'I always make that clear up front.'

'Is that your deal with Ro?'

'No,' he admitted. 'I don't think either of us expected this and, if you want me to be honest with you, we don't have a clue where this is going. We're taking it step by step. But I would never deliberately hurt her or the children. As far as the twins are concerned, Rosie's being kind and befriending me because I don't know many people in London.'

'Fair enough,' Daisy said.

'You won't have to pick up the pieces,' he assured her solemnly.

'Daze, are you grilling him?' Rosie asked, appearing in the doorway.

'Big sister's privilege.' Daisy sounded completely unrepentant.

'I'd be more worried if she didn't,' Leo said. 'It's fine. I think Daisy and I understand each other.'

'We do,' Daisy agreed. 'And I want to see this dress properly. That selfie you sent me from the changing rooms was hardly visible.'

'Bossy,' Rosie grumbled, but went to change into her new finery.

Daisy was duly impressed. 'Stunning. You know Lexi's going to say you need a crown because you look like a princess. I can't remember which one has the blue dress?'

Rosie groaned. 'Cinderella.'

'We've already established that I'm not Prince Charming and my car's not going to turn into a pumpkin at midnight,' Leo said. 'Plus you love her, Daisy, and you don't make her be a skivvy.'

Daisy grinned. 'But you have dark hair, like the original Prince Charming, and you're taking my sister to a ball. Are you going to have to wear a royal outfit with a sash and gold epaulettes?'

He groaned. 'No. I'm just a duke. It's standard white tie.'

'White tie's super-posh. Does that mean you wear a top hat? Or an opera cloak?' Daisy asked.

He laughed. 'Now you're making me sound like a pantomime villain. No. And there's no monocle, either.'

'Pity. Because I think Freddie would love to try on your top hat.'

'Freddie,' he countered, 'would much rather have a dinosaur outfit.'

Daisy smiled. 'That's true. Right. Enough grilling from me. Let's go and drink our coffee.'

Rosie seemed more relaxed around her sister, Leo noticed. And he liked this fun, teasing side of her. He rather thought that she brought out the best in him, too. So maybe this would work out, after all. And if his mother got on as well with Rosie as he thought she might, this weekend could be the start of their future.

CHAPTER EIGHT

ON SATURDAY MORNING, Leo drove over to Rosie's house. They fixed the children's car seats in the back of his car, then stowed their luggage in the boot and picked up Nina.

'We're going to Italy to eat ice cream,' Lexi informed Nina, bouncing in her seat.

'And we're going to see knights in armour, with swords,' Freddie said. 'We're staying in a real castle!'

Nina laughed. 'I can see just how much you two are looking forward to it. I'm looking after you tonight while Mummy and Leo go to the charity ball.'

'Mummy looks like a princess in her dress,' Lexi said. 'It's so pretty.'

'You can tell me all about princesses and knights on the way,' Nina said, 'and we can colour in some pictures.'

'Yay!' the children chorused.

Michael had always upgraded their seats when they travelled, Rosie remembered; luxurious as it had felt at the time, it wasn't the same league as travelling with the Duke of Calvanera. Just as Leo had promised, there was no waiting around at the airport. And the plane, although small, was beautifully appointed, with deep, comfortable seats and lots of leg room.

'I still can't quite get my head around the fact that your friend owns a plane,' she said to Leo.

The children were enthralled by their first flight, especially when the pilot told them over the intercom that they could take their seat belts off. Leo took the children to the window and lifted them up so they could both see the land below.

'All the houses are tiny!' Lexi said in awe.

'And the clouds are all big and fluffy,' Freddie said.

They were overawed by seeing the mountains, too. And then finally Leo strapped them back into their seats for the descent so they could land at Florence.

Again, there wasn't a lot of waiting around. There was a limousine waiting for them at the airport, with car seats already fitted for the children. Rosie noticed that the driver was wearing a peaked cap and livery; she wondered if he was one of Leo's staff, or whether he'd just hired a car and driver for the journey.

As they headed into the hills outside Florence, Leo told the twins all about what they were seeing, and answered all their excited questions. Rosie was glad that she didn't have to make conversation, because adrenaline was pumping round her system. Supposing Leo's mother didn't like her? Would it be a problem that Rosie already had children? What if she did or said something wrong at the ball tonight and caused some kind of diplomatic embarrassment?

The nearer they got to the *palazzo*, the more her nerves grew.

And she was near to hyperventilating when the car stopped in front of a wrought-iron security gate set into a large stone wall.

'Here we are,' Leo said cheerfully. He climbed out of the car and tapped a code into the keypad set into the wall, and the iron gates swung open.

There was a long drive flanked with tall cypress trees, and then the vista opened up to show the castle itself. It was a huge three-storey building made of honey-coloured stone with a tower at one corner. The tall, narrow windows with their pointed arches were spaced evenly among the facade, and there were colonnaded arches along the ground floor. The perfect fairy-tale castle, Rosie thought.

'Is that the princess's tower?' Lexi asked, pointing to the tower.

'No, it's my tower,' Leo said. 'My study is on the very top floor and the views are amazing. I have a bedroom and bathroom on the floor below it, and a sitting room on the floor below that.'

'So are you a prince?' Lexi asked.

He smiled. 'No. You know I'm a doctor because I work with your *mamma* at the hospital.'

'But you live in a castle. You must be a prince,' Lexi said.

'I'm a duke,' he said gently.

'What's a duke?' Freddie wanted to know.

'It's a bit like a prince,' Rosie said.

'I just don't wear a crown or robes or anything,' Leo said.

'But can you make people into knights?' Freddie asked.

'No.' Leo smiled at him. 'But I can show you some knights' armour, when we go inside.'

The front door opened as they got out of the car, and an older man with grey hair and wearing a top hat and tails came to meet them.

Leo made formal introductions. 'This is Carlo, who manages the house for me,' he said to Rosie, Nina and the children.

'*Buongiorno.* Welcome to the Palazzo di Calvanera,' Carlo said, removing his hat, and bowed stiffly. 'If there's anything you require, *signora*, *signorina*, please just ask.' He looked at Leo. 'Is your luggage in the car, Duca?'

Leo rolled his eyes. 'Carlo, you've called me Leo for the last thirty-odd years. That doesn't change just because we have guests—and did you borrow that outrageous outfit from your son's theatre company?'

'I might have done.' Carlo laughed. 'Leo, you're the Duca di Calvanera. Your butler is supposed to dress accordingly.'

Leo laughed back. 'And this is the twenty-first century, so dress codes are a thing of the past. I guess I should consider myself lucky that you didn't find some outlandish livery.'

'Gio had a great costume from *Twelfth Night*. I was tempted to borrow it,' Carlo admitted. 'Except his Malvolio is much thinner than I am. I couldn't even get the jacket on, let alone done up.' He bowed to Rosie again. 'My son Gio has a theatre company in Florence. Leo helped him start the business.'

Seeing the warmth between Leo and the older man, Rosie wasn't surprised that Leo had helped Carlo's son.

'Your *mamma* is in her usual sitting room with Violetta,' Carlo said to Leo. 'I'll bring the luggage in and ask Maria to arrange refreshments.'

'Thank you.'

'Welcome home, Leo. It's good to see you.' Carlo hugged him impulsively. 'It doesn't seem five minutes since you were the same height as this little *bambino* here.' He ruffled Freddie's hair.

Freddie immediately clung to Leo's leg and stared up at Carlo, wide-eyed.

'Sorry. He's a little shy,' Rosie said.

'No matter.' Carlo bent down so he was nearer to the children's height. 'What would you like to drink? Milk? Juice? Lemonade?'

'Milk, please,' Lexi said.

'Me, too,' Freddie whispered. 'Please.'

'Welcome to the *palazzo*,' Carlo said again, and ushered them inside.

The inside of the castle was equally grand. The entrance hall had marble columns and a marble chequered floor; the walls were dark red and hung with gold-framed pictures, while the ceiling had ornate plasterwork around the cornices and a painting in the centre. Rosie glanced around to see Venetian glass chandeliers, a suit of armour holding a massive pole-axe, a marble-topped gilt table bearing a huge arrangement of roses and an enormous grandfather clock.

Lexi looked delighted. 'It's just like the prince's castle in *Beauty and the Beast*.'

'You like *Beauty and the Beast*?' Leo asked.

Lexi nodded. 'And it's Mummy's favourite because Belle teaches the prince to be kind.'

'It's important to be kind,' Leo agreed.

Was he just being kind to her and the children? Rosie wondered. Or was there more to it than that?

At one end of the hall was a massive sweeping staircase with gilded railings and balusters.

Rosie could imagine the Duchesses walking down the stairs, hundreds of years ago, wearing long swishy dresses with wide skirts.

Right at that moment, she felt slightly intimidated. Even though Carlo had been very welcoming, this was way outside her normal life. She'd visited stately homes in the past, enjoying the glimpse into a world so different from her own, but now she was staying in an actual castle as a guest. A castle whose owner had kissed her until she was dizzy.

'Carlo said Mamma is in her sitting room,' Leo said. 'Come and meet her.'

Rosie took Freddie's hand and Nina took Lexi's hand, and they followed him through the corridor into the sitting room where his mother was waiting. The room had an ornate plasterwork ceiling, but the walls were an unexpectedly bright turquoise. The huge windows let in lots of light and gave a view over the formal garden at the back of the *palazzo*; the marble floor was covered with silk rugs, but what worried Rosie was the furniture. The upholstery was either old-gold velvet or regency gold and cream stripes; the material wouldn't take kindly to small sticky hands.

'Don't touch anything,' she whispered to Freddie and Lexi.

The twins looked almost as intimidated as she felt.

'Allow me to introduce you,' Leo said. 'Mamma, Violetta, don't get up.'

Rosie noticed the stick propped against the sofa next to Leo's mother, and could guess why Leo had just said that.

'This is Rosie, her friend Nina from the hospital nursery school, and Rosie's children Freddie and Lexi. Rosie, Nina, Freddie and Lexi—this is my mother, the Duchess of Calvanera, and her friend Violetta,' Leo finished.

'*Buongiorno, Duchessa. Buongiorno,* Signora Violetta.' Rosie made a deep curtsey, and Nina followed suit.

'*Bwun-gy-or-no,*' Freddie and Lexi said, with Freddie bowing and Lexi curtseying and nearly falling over when she lost her balance.

'My dears, it's so nice to meet you. And we don't stand on ceremony at the *palazzo*. Please, call me Beatrice, and you really don't have to curtsey to me,' Leo's mother said, to Rosie's immense surprise. Hadn't Leo said that when he'd brought previous girlfriends here, his parents had reacted badly? Then again, he'd also said that his father had been difficult but his mother was sweet.

'And please call me Violetta,' Violetta added with a smile.

'Thank you for having us to stay, Beatrice,' Rosie said.

'Yes, thank you,' Nina added.

'You are all most welcome. Refreshments, I think, Leo. Go to the kitchen and ask Maria to arrange it.'

'Carlo is arranging everything,' Leo said.

'I think you should go yourself, Leo,' Beatrice said, looking pointedly at the doorway.

Leo was a little wary of leaving Rosie alone with his mother and Violetta. Then again, his mother hadn't been the problem with Emilia, and the *palazzo* definitely wasn't the same place without his father's iron fist. His father certainly wouldn't have been happy about the changes to the sitting room from the original moody dark green to the much brighter, warmer turquoise. Or the fact that his wife spoke her mind nowadays. '*Sì*, Mamma,' he said, and left for the kitchen.

As he'd half expected, Maria greeted him as warmly as Carlo had, fussing over him. 'It's good to have you back, Leo,' she said. 'The *palazzo* needs you.' She gave him a pointed look. 'And children. This place needs the laughter of children.'

Carlo had obviously told his wife just who had arrived with Leo. 'Which is what it will have, this weekend.' And maybe Rosie's children would help to banish some of the ghosts here. He hoped.

Leo returned to his mother's sitting room, carrying a massive silver tray of tea, cake and small glasses of milk for the children, and discovered that Lexi was sitting on his mother's lap, talking animatedly about princesses and crowns. He had to hide a smile; he should have guessed that the little girl would be the one to break the ice, and that it would take about ten seconds for her shyness to dissolve into her usual confidence. Freddie, the shyer twin, was sitting next to his mother on the sofa and holding her hand very tightly.

'Carlo's taken the luggage upstairs,' he said, and deftly poured the tea.

He could see Rosie eyeing the glasses warily. No doubt she was panicking that the twins would either spill the milk everywhere or break the glasses. 'The glasses are sturdy,' he said quietly to her, 'and spills are easily mopped up. Stop worrying.'

'Freddie, Lexi, you need to sit really still while you drink your milk,' Rosie said, not looking in the slightest bit less worried.

He handed the children a glass each.

'Maria has made us some of her special *schiacciata alla Fiorentina*,' he said, gesturing to the cake. 'It's an orange sponge cake with powdered sugar on top.'

Rosie looked aghast, clearly worrying about sticky fingers.

'Leonardo spilled more crumbs over the furniture when he was little than I care to remember,' Beatrice said, 'so please don't worry about Lexi and Freddie spilling a few crumbs.'

'My daughter Lisetta, too,' Violetta said. 'She spilled blackcurrant all over that sofa over there.' She pointed to one of the regency striped sofas. 'They survive. Things clean up. Don't worry about sticky hands and spilled drinks.'

Rosie gave them both a grateful look.

The cake was still slightly warm and utterly delicious, and both children were scrupulously polite and careful, he noticed.

'Leo, why don't you show Rosie, Nina and the children round the *palazzo* while Violetta and I have another cup of tea? I'm sure Freddie will like to see our knights in armour.' Beatrice smiled at Rosie. 'I know it is the custom in Italy to drink coffee all day, but Leonardo introduced us to English tea some years ago and it's so refreshing in summer.'

'Thank you,' Rosie said.

'Knights and princesses!' Lexi said, and wriggled off Beatrice's lap, almost spilling the old lady's tea in the process.

'Lexi. Slow and calm, please,' Rosie said quietly. 'You nearly spilled Beatrice's tea just then.'

Lexi put a hand to her mouth in horror. 'Sorry,' she said.

'It's all right. Everything's exciting when you're little,' Beatrice said, ruffling her curls. 'And I think children should be heard as well as seen.'

Since when? Leo thought. When he'd grown up, the 'children should be seen and not heard' rule had been very much in evidence. The only real affection he'd been shown had been from his nanny, from Carlo—a much more junior servant in those days—and from Maria if he sneaked into the kitchens.

Then again, maybe that had been more his father's rule, and Beatrice had been as scared of her husband's mercurial temper as Leo had been. Certainly his mother seemed to have blossomed in widowhood. She was physically more frail, with her arthritis forcing her to use a stick, but mentally she seemed much stronger. Maybe his father had played the same nasty little games with her that he had with Leo, dangling the promise of love and then making it impossible to reach.

'Come with me,' Leo said, and showed Rosie and the children the other formal rooms. The dining room, with its polished table big enough to seat twenty; another sitting room; a ballroom with a slew of floor-to-ceiling windows and mirrors to double the light in the room; the room his staff used as the estate office during the week, the heavy old furniture teamed with very modern state-of-the-art computer equipment; the library, with its floor-to-ceiling shelves that Lexi announced was just like the one in *Beauty and the Beast*; the music room, with its spinet and harpsichord and baby grand piano.

Freddie gasped as Leo led them into the final room: the armoury. Suits of armour from various ages of the *palazzo* stood in a line, and instead of paintings on the walls there was a display of shields and swords.

'But that one's a *little* suit of armour,' Freddie said in awe, pointing to the child-sized suit of armour.

At the same age, Leo had been fascinated by the miniature suit of armour. His father had forbidden him to touch it, but the lure had been too great. The time Leo had been caught trying on the helmet, he'd been put on bread and water for three days for daring to disobey his father.

Well, he wasn't his father.

Deliberately, he walked towards the little suit and removed the helmet. 'This is ceremonial armour,' he explained. 'It was made for the son of one of the Dukes of Calvanera, a couple of hundred years ago. Do you want to try on the helmet?'

Freddie's eyes grew round. 'Can I? Please?'

'Sure.' Leo helped him put it on, then knelt down beside him. 'Time for a selfie, I think.'

'Me, too!' Lexi demanded.

Leo hid a grin when she swiftly added, 'Please.' No doubt Rosie had just reminded her about manners. 'Your turn, next,' he promised; and when she was wearing the helmet with the visor up he took a selfie of the two of them together.

Freddie was galloping on the spot, clearly pretending that he was a knight on a horse. Leo smiled and ruffled his hair before returning the helmet to the tiny suit of armour.

'Come and see upstairs,' he said, leading them back into the hall and up the wide sweeping staircase.

Portraits in heavy gilt frames hung on the walls of the staircase; clearly they were portraits of previous Dukes, because Rosie noticed that the fashions seemed to change and grow older, the higher they climbed. Which meant that the forbidding man in the very first portrait must've been Leo's father. Part of her wondered why he hadn't said as much; then again, the little he had told her about his father made her realise why they hadn't been close. Though she noticed that he didn't mention the next portrait up, either, which was presumably his grandfather; like Leo's father, the Duke looked stern and forbidding. Had all the Dukes of Calvanera been like that? In which case the *palazzo* must have felt more like a prison for a small child. She'd seen the expression on his face when his mother had talked about children being heard as well as seen; clearly his childhood hadn't been much fun.

The first-floor hall had a marble floor and another of the ornate painted ceilings, Rosie noticed. But the guest rooms turned out to be much simpler than the downstairs rooms; they had wooden floors and the walls were painted lemon or duck-egg-blue or eau-de-nil on the top half and white beneath the dado rail. The paintings still had heavy gilt frames, but they were of landscapes rather than people. French doors let light into the rooms, fluttering through white voile curtains.

'This is where you'll be sleeping tonight, Freddie and Lexi,' Leo said, showing them into a room with twin four-poster single beds.

'Oh, look, a princess bed!' Lexi said in delight, seeing the gauzy fabric draped at the head of one bed.

'And a prince bed,' he said with a smile, gesturing to the other one. 'Nina, I assumed you'd like to be next door, but if you don't like the room just let me know and we can move you to one you prefer.'

'It'll be just fine, thanks,' Nina said.

'The bedrooms all have their own bathrooms,' Leo said, and Rosie peeked in to see yet more marble on the floor, but the suite was plain white enamel and the gilt towel stand was relatively simple.

The next room was clearly Rosie's, because her dress was hanging up to let the packing creases fall out.

'Again, if you'd rather have a different room, just say,' Leo said.

'No. It's beautiful,' she said, meaning it.

'Can we see the tower?' Lexi asked.

'Sure.'

Leo's rooms were very different from the rest of the house, Rosie thought. He didn't show them his bedroom, but the walls of his sitting room were white and the furniture was much more modern than in the rest of the house, and the art-work was watercolours of the sky and the sea. The room at the top was his study; the walls were lined with books, but the desk was the same kind of light modern furniture they'd seen in his sit-ting room, and there was a state-of-the-art com-puter on his desk.

'And you need to see out of the window,' he said, lifting both twins up so they could see.

'You can see nearly to the edge of the world,' Freddie said in awe.

'Well, to the hills in Tuscany,' Leo corrected with a smile.

A tour of the gardens was next.

'We've finished our tea, now,' Beatrice said, 'so we'll join you.' She struggled to her feet, wav-ing away Leo's offer of assistance, and steadied herself with her stick. 'I'm a little slower than I'd like to be, so I'll only walk with you as far as the roses,' she said.

'Thank you, Mamma,' Leo said.

Violetta took Beatrice's other arm, and the two older ladies led the way.

As soon as they were outside, Leo crouched down to Lexi and Freddie's level. 'You know

Mummy has rules at the playground? I have rules here. You can run around as much as you like on the grass, but you don't go anywhere near the lake without Mummy, Nina or me holding your hand, OK?'

'OK,' the twins chorused solemnly.

'And the same goes for the fountain in the middle of the garden. You need to stay three big jumps away from it, unless one of us is holding your hand.'

Rosie loved the fact that he'd put the children's safety first, and explained it to them in a way they could understand.

As they walked along, her hand brushed against his. The light contact made all her nerve-endings zing. It would be so easy just to let his fingers curl round hers, but that wasn't appropriate right now—not in front of her children, his mother, Violetta and Nina. She glanced at him and he was clearly thinking the same, because he mouthed, 'Later.'

Later they would be dancing cheek-to-cheek at the ball. Desire sizzled at the base of her spine at the thought of it. She could imagine walking here through this garden with him when they got home, the warm night air scented with roses. And he'd kiss her with every step…

She shook herself, realising that Beatrice was telling them about the flowers and the fountain in the centre of the rose garden.

'This is so lovely,' she said. 'Do you ever open the gardens to the public?'

Beatrice shook her head.

'Maybe you should,' Violetta said. 'It would be good for the house to have visitors. You could have a little *caffè*, too.'

'It would be an excellent idea, Mamma,' Leo agreed.

'Perhaps. We'll wait here for you,' Beatrice said, and sat down on one of the stone benches by the fountain.

Leo took them to see the lake; once they'd finished their tour of the garden, they collected Beatrice and Violetta, then sat on the terrace at the back of the house in the shade, and Carlo brought them a tray of cold drinks.

'Can we play ball?' Lexi asked.

'Sure,' Leo said, and took the children into the middle of the lawn.

'Thank you,' Beatrice said to Rosie. 'It's so

good to see my son looking relaxed and happy—
and I know it's down to you.'

How much did she know? Flustered, and not
wanting to make things difficult for Leo, Rosie
said, 'We're just friends.'

'That's not the way you look at each other,
child,' Beatrice said.

Rosie bit her lip. 'I wasn't sure you'd approve of
me being Leo's girlfriend. I'm not from a noble
family, and I already have two children.'

'That doesn't matter—and it's a pleasure to
hear children laughing here.' Beatrice looked
sad. 'It didn't happen as often as it should have
when Leonardo was growing up.'

Leo had said his father was difficult, Rosie remembered.

Beatrice took her hand and squeezed it. 'As a
mamma, all you want is to see your child happy,
yes?'

'And you worry about them all the time,' Rosie
agreed.

'I think we understand each other,' Beatrice
said softly. 'And I'm glad he brought you here.'

So maybe, if this thing between her and Leo

worked out the way Rosie was starting to hope it might, his family wouldn't object…

After Leo had tired the children out playing ball, they came back to sit in the shade.

'Why don't you have a dog?' Lexi asked.

'Lexi—that's rude,' Rosie said gently.

'No, it's fine. I don't have a dog because I'm too old,' Beatrice said. 'You can't take a dog for a proper walk when you have to walk with a stick. Not even a little dog.'

'We don't have a dog because Mummy works,' Freddie said dolefully.

'Let's do some colouring,' Rosie said, hoping to head them off.

Nina took pads of drawing paper and crayons from her bag. 'You can do a nice picture of the castle,' she said.

But, as Rosie half expected, both children drew their favourite picture: a dog.

'This is for you,' Lexi said, giving her picture to Beatrice. 'It's a dog but you don't have to take it for walks.'

'And I drawed you one, too, so you have two and they won't be lonely,' Freddie said, not to be outdone.

Beatrice was close to tears as she hugged them. 'Thank you, both of you.'

'Maybe you can sing a song for Beatrice and Violetta,' Nina suggested. 'Like you do at nursery school.'

When the twins had finished their song, Beatrice smiled. 'This reminds me of my Leonardo singing songs, when he was little.'

'He singed to us last week,' Lexi confided.

'He sings a lot,' Freddie added.

'Maybe you should indulge your *mamma* and the children, Leo, and sing to us now,' Violetta suggested with a smile.

He groaned. 'I don't have any choice, do I?' But he gave in with good grace and sang some traditional Italian songs.

This felt magical, Rosie thought, but she was still aware that this opulent, privileged world was nothing like her everyday existence. So she would let herself enjoy every second of the weekend, but she would keep in the back of her mind that this was just a holiday and she shouldn't get used to it. She and the children belonged in their tiny little terrace in London, not a duke's castle in Tuscany.

'So what is the children's routine?' Beatrice asked later.

'They usually eat at half-past five or so, and then have a bath before bed,' Rosie said.

'The ball starts at eight,' Leo said, 'and it will take us about half an hour to get there.'

'It won't take me long to get ready,' Rosie reassured him.

'I'm here to take care of the children,' Nina reminded them.

'And perhaps I can read a bedtime story,' Beatrice said. 'It's been a long time since I've read a goodnight story. Too long. I miss that.'

Was that his mother's subtle way of reminding him that he was supposed to get married and have an heir? Leo wondered. Then again, maybe she was just lonely and enjoying the chance to have some temporary grandchildren. She certainly seemed to have taken the twins to her heart, which gave him hope.

'Nina, I hope you will eat with Violetta and me tonight,' Beatrice said. 'Maria has planned something special for tonight.'

Nina went pink with pleasure. 'Thank you.'

Again, it showed Leo how different the *palazzo*

was now. Under his father's rule, Nina would've been banished to the nursery with the children and treated as a servant.

Maria had made garlic bread shaped like teddy bears for the children, served with pasta and followed by ice cream. And she insisted that Rosie and Leo should have some *piadinas*, toasted flatbreads filled with cheese and ham. 'You can't dance all night on an empty stomach.' She waved her hand in disgust. 'The food's always terrible at a ball, all soggy canapés and crumbly things you can't eat without ruining your clothes. You need to eat something now.'

'Thank you, Maria,' Leo said, giving her a hug.

When they'd finished eating, Nina waved Rosie away. 'I'll do bathtime. Go and get ready—the children will want to see you all dressed up, and so do I.'

Rosie knew it would be pointless arguing, so she did as she was told and then headed for the children's bedroom.

'Look! Mummy's just like a princess,' Lexi said in delight.

'A special princess,' Freddie added.

Rosie smiled. 'Thank you.'

'But there's something missing,' Beatrice said thoughtfully. 'Violetta, I wonder, can you help me?'

The two older women left the room, and returned carrying some small leather and gilt boxes.

Rosie gasped when Beatrice opened the boxes to reveal a diamond choker, earrings and bracelet.

'These will be perfect with that dress. Try them on,' Beatrice said.

'But—but—these are *real* diamonds.' Put together, they were probably worth more than she'd ever earn over the course of her entire lifetime, Rosie thought.

'Diamonds are meant to be worn, not stuck in a safe. I'm too old to go to a ball and I can't dance any more, not with my stick,' Beatrice said. 'So perhaps you can wear these for me, tonight.'

Warily, Rosie tried them on.

The jewels flashed fire at her reflection and made her feel like a million dollars.

'But what if I lose them?' she asked.

'They're insured,' Beatrice said. 'But you won't lose them—will she, Leo?'

'Of course she won't,' Leo said, entering the

twins' room, and Rosie caught her breath. He looked amazing in a tailcoat, formal trousers and white tie, shirt and waistcoat.

'You have to take selfies,' Lexi said.

'I agree,' Beatrice said, and produced a state-of-the-art mobile phone. 'Use this. I will send you the pictures later.'

What could Rosie do but agree?

'Put your arm round Rosie's shoulder, Leo,' Violetta directed.

The touch of Leo's hand against her bare shoulder made desire shimmer through Rosie.

'Bellissima.' Beatrice smiled and took the photograph. 'Now off you go to the ball, and have a wonderful time.'

CHAPTER NINE

LEO DROVE THEM in to Florence in a sleek, low-slung black car—the kind of car Rosie had only ever really seen in magazines.

When she said as much, he gave her a rueful smile. 'I know I see myself more as a doctor than as a duke, but I have to admit that cars like this are my weakness. And it's the privileged bit of my life that pays for this.'

'But you don't spend all the money on yourself. We're going to a charity ball tonight,' she reminded him, 'in aid of a clinic you support financially. And Carlo said you supported his son's theatre company.'

'It's important to give something back.'

Rosie had a feeling that his mother might agree with him, but his father definitely hadn't. Though now wasn't the time to bring up the subject. Instead, she said, 'Right now I really feel like Cinderella. Is this car going to turn into a pumpkin at midnight?'

Leo laughed. 'No, but you look beautiful and this is going to be fun.'

And it was going to be just the two of them.

Well, and a lot of people that Leo knew either professionally or in his capacity as the Duke of Calvanera.

But tonight she'd get to dance with him; and for those few moments it would be just them and the night and the music.

While Leo parked the car, Rosie called Nina to check that everything was OK. Reassured, she went into the ball, holding Leo's arm.

The hotel was one of the swishest in Florence, overlooking the River Arno. Like the *palazzo* in the mountains, the building was very old, but had been brought up to date. The ballroom was even more luxurious than the one at Calvanera, as well as being much larger; it had a high ceiling with ornate mouldings, painted in golds and creams. The floor-to-ceiling windows had voile curtains and heavy green velvet drapes; mirrors between the windows reflected even more light from the glass and gold chandeliers hanging from the ceiling and the matching sconces on the walls.

'This room's amazing,' she said.

'Isn't it just?' Leo agreed.

And everyone was dressed appropriately, the men in white tie and the women in an array of gorgeous dresses. Rosie had never seen anything so glamorous in her entire life.

A jazz trio was playing quietly on the dais at one end of the room.

'Dance with me,' Leo said, 'and then I'll introduce you to everyone.'

It had been quite a while since Rosie had been dancing, and Leo was a spectacular dancer; as he waltzed her round the room, it felt as if she were floating on air. And being in his arms felt perfect. Like coming home.

He introduced her to a stream of people, explaining that she was on the team with him at Paddington Children's Hospital in London; just as he'd reassured her earlier in the week, everyone spoke perfect English, and Rosie felt slightly guilty that all she really knew in Italian was *please*, *thank you*, *hello* and *goodbye*. Nobody seemed to mind; and, although she ended up talking mostly about medicine, she didn't feel as out of place as she'd half expected to be.

'Leo, can you excuse me for a second?' she asked after a quick glance at her watch.

'I know. You need to check on the children.' Though he wasn't mocking her; she knew he understood why she was antsy.

She went out to the terrace, where it was a little quieter, to make the call. Nina confirmed that everything at the *palazzo* was just fine—there hadn't been a peep out of either twin.

Rosie had just ended the call, slipped her phone back into her evening bag and was about to head back into the ballroom to find Leo when a man standing near to her on the terrace fell to the floor in a crumpled heap.

A woman screamed and knelt down beside the man—presumably his wife—and Rosie said to her, 'I'm a nurse—can I help?'

'Mi scusi?'

Oh, no. Just when she really needed not to have a language barrier, she'd found one of the few people here who didn't speak English.

She gestured to the man, then clutched a fist to her heart, miming squeezing, and hoped that either he or the woman would realise that she was asking if he thought he'd had a heart attack.

'*Mi ha punto una vespa.*' He pointed to his hand.

Vespa? Wasn't that a motorcycle? She didn't have a clue what he'd just said.

'*Una vespa.*' His wife mimed flapping wings.

He seemed to be having problems breathing and was wheezing; and then Rosie's nursing training kicked in as she noticed the reddened area on his hand. He'd clearly been stung, or bitten by an insect, and was having a severe allergic reaction.

'Do you have adrenaline?' she asked, hoping that the Italian word was similar to the English one.

'Adrenaline?' The woman frowned and shook her head.

Rosie grabbed her phone and called Leo, who answered within two rings. 'Rosie? Is something wrong with the children?'

'No. I'm on the terrace with a man I think is having a severe allergic reaction to a sting. He and his wife don't speak English but between us we worked out they don't have adrenaline. I need you to talk to them for me to find out his medical history, for someone to ring an ambulance and for someone to put a call out to everyone at the ball in case someone else has an adrenaline pen we can borrow.' She handed the phone to the woman. 'Speak to Leo, *per favore*?'

There were glasses on a nearby table containing ice as well as the drinks; she grabbed a tissue from her bag and gestured to the ice. *'Per favore?'* she asked the people standing round the table. At the assorted nods, she grabbed the ice, put it in the tissue and put the makeshift ice pack on the man's hand. Gently, she got him to lie back on the terrace, and talked to him to keep him calm. 'It's going to be all right,' she said, knowing that he wouldn't understand what she was saying, but hoping he could pick up on her tone.

The man's wife finished talking to Leo and handed the phone back to Rosie.

'Grazie,' Rosie said. 'Leo?'

'His name's Alessandro and hers is Caterina. He's been stung before and the swelling was bad but he didn't think to talk to his doctor about it. The last time must have sensitised him, because he's never had an anaphylactic reaction before,' Leo explained. 'I've got an ambulance on its way and I've got a call out in the ballroom for an adrenaline pen.'

'Great. Thank you. How do I say "Everything will be OK"?'

'Andrà tutto bene,' he said. 'I'll be there as soon as I've found an adrenaline pen.'

'Thanks.' She hung up and squeezed Alessandro's hand and Caterina's in turn. 'Alessandro, Caterina, *andrà tutto bene,*' she said. 'Everything will be fine. An ambulance is coming.'

'Grazie,' Caterina said, looking close to tears. She, too, talked to Alessandro; Rosie didn't have a clue what she was saying, but Caterina's tone was reassuring and she was clearly trying to be brave and calm for her husband's sake.

To Rosie's relief, Leo arrived a couple of minutes later with an adrenaline pen. While he explained to Caterina and Alessandro why Rosie had laid him flat and put an ice pack over the sting, and what was going to happen next, Rosie glanced at her watch and then administered the adrenaline.

She really wasn't happy with Alessandro's

breathing, and when he was still struggling five minutes after she'd given the first injection, she gave him a second shot.

Finally, the ambulance arrived. Leo spoke to the paramedics to fill them in on what had happened; then they carried Alessandro off on a stretcher with Caterina accompanying him.

'You saved his life,' Leo said.

'Not just me. You talked to Caterina, you got someone to call the ambulance and you got the adrenaline pen.'

'But you saw what the problem was. Without you working that out, it might have been too late by the time the ambulance got here,' Leo said. He held her close. 'You, Rosie Hobbes, are officially a superstar.'

She shook her head. 'I'm just an ordinary nurse.'

'Ordinary is definitely not how I'd describe you,' Leo said. 'Caterina's going to ring me from the hospital and let me know how Alessandro gets on.'

'That's good.' She bit her lip. 'Talking of calling...'

'Of course. You need to check on the children.'

He stroked her face. 'Come and find me when you're done.'

'Thank you.' She called Nina. 'Is everything OK?'

'It's fine,' Nina said. 'Honestly, Rosie, you don't need to worry. You know I'll call you if there's a problem. I have Leo's number as well as yours and that of the hotel reception, and I'm sleeping right next door to the children—so if one of them wakes up I'll hear them straight away.'

'Sorry. I do trust you. I'm just one of these really terrible overprotective mums,' Rosie said.

'Just a bit,' Nina said, though her tone was gentle. 'I hope you don't mind, but I'm not planning to stay up until you get back. Violetta has gone home and Beatrice has gone to bed, and I'm going to read in my room for a bit. So just try to relax and enjoy the ball, OK?'

'OK,' Rosie said. 'And thank you.'

She went to find Leo and relayed the conversation to him.

'She has a point,' he said with a smile. 'You need to relax and enjoy this. Come and dance with me.'

Just having him there with her made her feel better, and Rosie finally managed to relax in his arms.

As she'd promised, Caterina rang from the hospital to tell Leo that Alessandro was recovering and would be sent home in the morning, along with an adrenaline pen that he'd make sure was with him at all times.

When the music slowed and the lights dimmed, Leo held Rosie close. And there in the ballroom, swaying to the music, it felt as if nobody else was there: just the two of them.

At the end of the evening, Leo drove them back to the *palazzo*. Although someone—presumably Carlo—had left the light on by the front door and in the hallway, Rosie was pretty sure that everyone in the *palazzo* was asleep.

'There's a full moon,' Leo said quietly, gesturing to the sky. 'And I'm not ready to go to bed yet. Come and walk with me for a while in the gardens.'

'Do you mind if I take my shoes off?' Rosie asked when he led her onto the lawn. 'I'm not used to wearing heels this high.'

'Sure,' he said, and let her lean on him while

she removed the strappy high heels and placed them on one of the stone benches.

Every single one of Rosie's senses felt magnified as they walked hand in hand through the gardens. In the moonlight, the garden looked magical; beneath her feet, the lawn felt like velvet. She could smell the sweet, drowsy scent of the roses, and in the distance she could hear a bird singing.

'Is that a nightingale?' she asked.

'I think so.' He stopped and spun her into his arms. 'Dance with me, Rosie,' he whispered.

Instead of the jazz band, they had the nightingale; instead of the chandeliers, they had the moon and the stars; and there was nobody to disturb them in their makeshift ballroom.

She closed her eyes as Leo held her close and dipped his head so he could brush his mouth against hers. Every nerve-end was begging for more, and she let him deepen the kiss; his mouth was teasing and inciting rather than demanding, and she found herself wanting more and more.

'Rosie,' he whispered when he finally broke the kiss. 'I want you.'

'I want you, too,' she admitted.

'Come to the tower with me?' he asked.

'I need to check on the children first.'

'What if you wake them? Or Nina?' he asked.

'I won't.' But she needed to see them.

'OK. Let's do this,' he said softly. He scooped her up, stopping only at the stone bench to pick up her shoes, and carried her back to the *palazzo*.

He set her on her feet again and kissed her before unlocking the door and dealing with the alarm system. And then he reset it and led her to the children's room.

The night-light was faint but enough to show her that they were both curled up under their duvets. She smiled and bent down to them in turn, breathing in the scent of their hair and kissing their foreheads lightly, so as not to wake them.

Just seeing them safe made her feel grounded again.

'I'm sorry,' she whispered when they'd left the children and were heading for the tower. 'I know they're perfectly safe here and I'm being ridiculous.'

'But Michael's associate really frightened you.'

She nodded. 'It's so hard to get past that.'

'It's OK. I understand.' He scooped her up

again. 'But now it's you and me. Just for a little while.'

Could she do this?

Could she put herself first—just for a little while?

When he kissed her again, she said, 'Yes.'

Leo's bedroom in the tower was so high up that he knew nobody would be able to see into the room. Moonlight filtered in through the soft voile curtains at the windows; he led Rosie over to the window, leaving the heavy drapes where they were, and pushed the voile aside for a moment. 'You, me and the moonlight,' he said, and kissed her bare shoulder.

She shivered, and slowly he lowered the zip of her dress. Her skin was so soft, so creamy in the moonlight. He turned her to face him, cupped her face in his hands and dipped his head so he could brush his mouth against hers, then pulled back so he could look into her eyes. Her pupils were huge, making her eyes look almost black.

'I want you,' he whispered. So badly that it was a physical ache.

'I want you too,' she answered, her voice slightly hoarse.

He slid the straps of her dress down and kissed her bare shoulders. When he felt her shiver, he paused. 'OK?'

'Very OK. Don't stop.'

He drew the gauzy material down further, then dropped to his knees and kissed her bare midriff. She slid her fingers into his hair. 'Leo.'

He wanted everything. Now. And yet the anticipation was just as exciting. He helped her step out of the dress, then hung the garment over the back of a chair.

She stood there before him wearing only a strapless lacy bra, matching knickers, and diamonds.

He sucked in a breath. 'Do you have any idea how sexy you look right now?'

'I just feel underdressed,' she confessed, a blush stealing through her cheeks.

He spread his hands. 'Then do something about it, *bellezza*.'

'*Bellezza?*'

'In my language it means "beautiful",' he explained.

'Oh.' Her blush deepened; and then she gave him a smile so sexy that it almost drove him to his knees. 'You're beautiful, too,' she whispered. 'And I want to see you.'

'Do it,' he said, his voice cracking with need and desire.

Slowly, so slowly, she removed his jacket and hung it over the top of her dress. Then she undid his waistcoat, slid it from his shoulders and draped it over the top of his jacket.

Leo was dying to feel her hands against his bare skin; but at the same time he was enjoying the anticipation and he didn't want to rush her. The tip of her tongue caught between her teeth as she concentrated on undoing his bow tie, then unbuttoned his shirt. He could feel the warmth of her hands through the soft cotton, and it made him want more. He couldn't resist stealing a kiss as she pushed the material off his shoulders and let the shirt fall to the floor.

Then he caught his breath as finally he felt her fingertips against his skin.

'Nice pecs, Dr Marchetti,' she murmured. She let her hands drift lower. 'Nice abs, too.' She gave him a teasing smile, and excitement hummed through him. Where would she touch him next? How?

And he wanted to touch her. So much that he couldn't hold himself back; he traced the lacy edge of her bra with his fingertips. 'Nice curves,' he said huskily, and was rewarded with a sharp intake of breath from her.

Her hands were shaking slightly as she undid the buckle of his belt, then the button of his trousers.

'OK?' he asked.

'It's been a while,' she admitted. 'I guess a part of me's a bit scared I'll—well—disappoint you.'

How could she possibly be worried about that? 'You're not going to disappoint me,' he reassured her. 'And I didn't plan this. Tonight really was all about just dancing with you and having fun.'

'I wasn't planning this to happen, either.' Her eyes widened. 'I don't have any protection. I'm not on the Pill.'

'I have protection,' he said. 'But I don't want you to think I'm taking you for granted.'

In answer she kissed him, and he felt his control snap.

He wasn't sure which of them finished undressing each other, but the next thing he knew he'd dropped the diamonds on his dressing table and had carried her to his bed, and she was lying with her head tipped back into his pillows, smiling up at him.

'I've wanted you since the moment I first saw you,' he whispered.

'Even though I was horrible to you?'

'Even though.' He stole a kiss. 'I don't know what it was. Your gorgeous eyes. Your mouth. Your hair. But something about you drew me and I want you. Very, very badly.'

'I want you, too,' she confessed.

She reached up and kissed him back. When he broke the kiss, he could see that her mouth was slightly swollen and reddened from kissing him, and her eyes glittered with pure desire. It was good to know she was with him all the way.

He kissed the hollows of her collarbones, then let his mouth slide lower. She gasped when he took one nipple into his mouth; he teased it with the tip of his tongue until her breathing had grown deeper and less even. Then he stroked her midriff and moved lower, kissing his way down her body and circling her navel with his tongue. He loved the feel of her curves, so soft against his skin.

'Bellezza,' he whispered. 'You're so beautiful, Rosie.'

'So are you,' she said shyly, sliding her hands along his shoulders.

He kneeled back so he could look at her, sprawled on his bed. His English rose. And now he wanted to see her lose that calmness and un-flappability he was used to at work. He wanted to see passion flare in her.

Keeping his gaze fixed on hers, he let his fin-gertips skate upwards from her knees. She caught her breath and parted her thighs, letting him touch her more intimately.

'Yes, Leo,' she whispered. 'Now.'

He reached over to the drawers next to his bed, took a condom from the top drawer, undid the foil packet and slid the condom on.

Then he kissed her again and whispered, 'Open your eyes, Rosie.'

When she did so, he eased his body into hers, watching the way the colour of her eyes changed.

She gasped, and wrapped her legs round him so he could push deeper.

He could feel the softness of her breasts against his chest, the hardness of her nipples.

'You feel like paradise,' he whispered.

'So do you.' Colour bloomed in her cheeks.

He held her closer, and began to move. His blood felt as if it were singing through his veins.

'Leo.' He felt her tighten round him as her climax hit, and it pushed him into his own climax.

Regretfully, he withdrew. 'Please don't go just yet,' he said. 'I need to deal with everything in the bathroom—but I'm not ready for you to leave just yet.'

'I'll stay,' she promised.

When Leo came back from the bathroom, Rosie was still curled in his bed, though she'd pulled the sheet over herself and she blushed when she saw that he was still completely naked.

He climbed into bed beside her and pulled her into his arms. 'Stay a little longer?'

He liked just lying there, holding her, with her head resting on his shoulder and his arm wrapped round her waist. There wasn't any need to make small talk; he just felt completely in tune with her. He couldn't remember ever feeling this happy before at the *palazzo*.

Rosie and the children really fitted in, here. He'd resisted the idea of having a family in Tuscany, not wanting to subject a child to the kind of misery he'd known here. But he wasn't his father; so maybe this place could actually house a happy family.

His last thought before he drifted into sleep was that maybe he, Rosie and the twins could be a family here...

CHAPTER TEN

NEXT MORNING ROSIE WOKE, warm and comfortable and with a body spooned against hers. When she realised that she was still in Leo's bed, she was horrified. She'd only meant to stay for a little while—not for the whole night. Supposing the children had woken from a bad dream, needed her and found her missing?

'Leo. *Leo*,' she whispered urgently. 'I need to go back to my room before the children wake up.'

And she hadn't even bothered taking off her make-up last night. She probably looked like a panda this morning—a panda with a bad case of bed-head.

'With a combination of lots of fresh air and all that running around yesterday, they're probably still asleep,' he pointed out, and kissed her. 'Good morning, *bellezza*.'

Oh, help.

When he spoke in his own language to her, it

made her knees go weak. And that sensual look in his eyes… Panicking, she began, 'Leo, I don't normally—'

He cut her off by pressing a finger gently to her lips. 'No apologies. Last night was last night. We didn't plan it.' He held her gaze. 'But I don't have any regrets.'

She could see by his face that he meant it.

Did she have regrets?

Yes and no.

She didn't regret making love with him. He'd made her feel wonderful. But it was way too tempting to let herself believe that this thing between them could turn from a fairy tale to real life. And she knew that couldn't happen. He needed to marry someone from his world and produce an heir to the dukedom.

'Thank you,' she said. 'But I really do have to go now.' She bit her lip. 'If you don't mind, I could do with a hand zipping up my dress.'

'I've got a better idea. I'll lend you a bathrobe,' he said. 'It'll be quicker. And I'll see you back to your room and carry your dress.'

'What if people see us?' she asked, worrying. She wasn't ashamed of what they'd done; but she didn't want people knowing about it. This was just between them. *Private.* And she needed some time to process it. To think about where they could possibly go from here. She couldn't do that if everyone knew about it.

'They won't,' he said, 'but if anyone sees me on the way back from your room I'll tell them I went outside for some fresh air before my shower.' He stroked her face. 'The *palazzo* is a little bit like a warren, and the least I can do is see you safely back to your room.'

It made sense. Otherwise she was at risk of going into the wrong room and embarrassing herself even further.

She shrugged on the fluffy white bathrobe he held out for her. It was way too big for her, but she tied the belt tightly.

He wrapped a towel round his waist, sarong-style; it looked incredibly sexy, and she had a hard job reminding herself that they were supposed to be just colleagues.

Except last night they'd been lovers.

'You need these, too.' Leo handed her the diamonds and she put them carefully in the deep pockets of his robe.

He carried her dress and shoes, and thankfully they didn't bump into anyone on the way back to her room. She put the jewels on the dressing table, then gave the bathrobe back to him.

Leo smiled and stole a kiss. 'I'll see you at breakfast, then. Do you know how to get to the breakfast room?'

'Down the stairs and then turn right?' she guessed.

He nodded. 'See you in a bit.'

Rosie hung up her dress, showered and dressed swiftly, then went into the children's room. They were just waking up and gave her the sweetest smiles.

'Mummy!' Freddie exclaimed. 'We missed you.'

'I missed you, too. I love you,' she told them both, and hugged them fiercely.

'Were there any princes and princesses at the ball?' Lexi wanted to know.

'No, but there were some very pretty dresses.'

'Did you take selfies?' Lexi asked.

'No.' She ruffled her daughter's hair. 'I need to get you both up now. We have to go down to breakfast.'

Rosie had just finished helping them get dressed when Nina came in. 'Sorry. I wasn't sure if they'd be awake yet.'

'It's fine. You're not supposed to be on duty twenty-four-seven,' Rosie said with a smile. 'I'll read them a story while you get ready, and we can all go down together.'

'That sounds good. Did you have fun last night?' Nina asked.

'Yes. The ball was great. And it really helped knowing that you were here with the children. Thanks so much for that.'

'No problem. They were angels.'

Once Nina was ready, they made their way to the breakfast room: a sunny room overlooking the terrace. Beatrice and Leo were already there.

'Good morning,' Beatrice said. 'Did you sleep well?'

Rosie didn't dare meet Leo's gaze. 'Very well, thank you.'

'Coffee, *signor, signorina*?' Carlo asked. 'And hot chocolate for the children?'

'That would be lovely, thanks,' Rosie said.

'Help yourself to pastries and *biscotti*,' Leo said. 'We tend to have a very light breakfast in Italy,'

Beatrice said, 'but Maria can make you bacon and egg, if you prefer.'

'This is all perfect,' Rosie said with a smile. 'And thank you for the loan of your diamonds.' She returned the boxes to Beatrice.

'My pleasure, my dear,' Beatrice said. 'Now, tell me all about the ball.'

Rosie focused on the dancing and the dresses—but Leo had his own story to tell.

'She saved a man's life last night, Mamma,' he said. 'He was stung by a wasp and had a very bad allergic reaction. Thanks to Rosie, he made it to hospital and he'll make a full recovery.'

'It wasn't just me,' Rosie said, squirming. 'I couldn't have done it without you translating for me, and getting the ambulance and the adrenaline.'

'But if you hadn't noticed what the problem was,' he said gently, 'Alessandro might have died.' He smiled at Freddie and Lexi. 'Your mummy is amazing.'

'That's what Aunty Daze says,' Lexi confided.

Violetta arrived after breakfast; they spent the rest of the morning in the gardens, with the children running round and playing ball with Leo. A couple of times, she caught his eye and wondered if he was remembering last night, when the two of them had danced barefoot in the moonlight among the roses.

On the way back to the airport, Leo switched on his phone and a slew of messages flooded in.

He grimaced and handed his phone to her.

The *Celebrity Life!* magazine website had run a report on the charity ball last night, asking who the beautiful woman was with the Duke of Calvanera—especially as she was wearing the Calvanera diamonds. Had someone finally caught the reluctant Duke?

There was a newer story attached to it: *Angel in Diamonds*. All about how she'd been a ministering angel to a man suffering from a near-fatal allergy to wasps, and saved his life.

Oh, no.

She grimaced and mouthed, 'Sorry.'

'It gets worse,' he mouthed back, and her dismay grew when he leaned over and flicked into a second website.

The journalists had dug up her past.

Rosie Hobbes, a twenty-five-year-old mother of twins, is a nurse at the beleaguered Paddington Children's Hospital. She was previously married to Michael Duncan, who died after his car collided with a tree, leaving a mountain of gambling debts.

Rosie stared at the screen, horrified, and totally shocked that her private life had been spilled over the press so quickly.

And then the fear seeped in.

What if Michael's former associates saw all this and decided that Leo, as the Duke of Calvanera, had plenty of money? Supposing they came after him, or threatened the children again? And Leo's mother was vulnerable at the *palazzo*, being elderly and frail. Although Violetta, Carlo and Maria would be with her, Rosie knew, would they be enough to keep her safe?

She didn't even know where to start asking questions, but looked helplessly at Leo.

'My PR team is doing damage limitation,' he said grimly.

'What's wrong?' Nina asked.

'Nothing,' Rosie fibbed—then grabbed her own phone from her bag and texted Nina.

Press gossip about me, things I don't want the children to hear but you probably need to know. Am sorry I didn't say anything before.

She sent Nina the link to the two articles.

'That'll probably be a text from my mum asking if I'm going to be home for tea tonight,' Nina said when her phone beeped.

Thankfully the children were too young to read many of the words, Rosie thought.

A few minutes later, Nina texted her back.

Poor you. Not fair of them to drag it all up. You OK?

Rosie sagged with relief; at least this wasn't going to be a problem at the hospital nursery school. She also knew that Nina wasn't a gossip.

I'm fine, she fibbed. Thanks for keeping it to yourself.

Try not to worry, Nina responded. Let me know if there's anything I can do. Thanks.

Leo was busy on his phone—Rosie assumed he

was dealing with his PR team—but he reached over to squeeze her hand, as if telling her that everything was going to be all right.

But the more she thought about it, the more she realised that it wasn't going to be all right. She was completely unsuitable for him. The press would bring up her past over and over and over again, and he'd be tainted by association. Beatrice had been so kind and welcoming this weekend; but right now Rosie felt as if she'd thrown all that back in Beatrice's face.

Nina kept the children occupied with stories and singing and colouring all the way back to England, so they weren't aware that anything was wrong. And thankfully they fell asleep in the car so there weren't any awkward questions.

Leo dropped Nina home first but, when he was about to turn into Rosie's road, they could see a group of people waiting at the front of Rosie's house.

'The paparazzi,' he said with a sigh.

'But how do they even know where I live?' Rosie asked, shocked.

He groaned. 'Sorry. They can dig up practically anything. I should have thought about this earlier.' He drove past her road. 'You'd better stay at mine.'

'They're probably camped out there, too,' she said. 'Maybe you'd better drop us on the next road. We can cut through the back.'

'I can't just abandon you.'

'You're not abandoning me. You're dropping us off at a place where we can walk through to the back of my house unseen.'

'I don't like this,' Leo said.

'It's the only option,' she said firmly.

'One condition, then,' he said. 'You let me know you're home safely, and you call me if there's any kind of problem at all.'

'OK,' she promised.

She woke the children. 'We're going to play a game, now,' she said. 'We're going to pretend to be invisible, so we have to tiptoe home.'

'Yay!' Lexi said, then screwed up her face and whispered, 'Yay.'

Rosie couldn't help smiling. 'Say goodbye and thank you to Leo.'

'Bye-bye and thank you,' the twins chorused.

Thankfully they managed to get in the back door without incident, and Rosie shepherded

the children upstairs. At least one of the waiting press must've seen a movement through the
frosted glass panel of the front door, because the
doorbell went, but Rosie ignored it.

Safely indoors, she texted Leo.

Going to put the children to bed.

Call me later, he texted back immediately.

Rosie continued to ignore the doorbell and ran
a bath for the children.

'Mummy, it's the doorbell,' Freddie said. 'It
might be the postman.'

'Not on a Sunday. Whoever it is can come back
later,' Rosie said firmly, 'because I'm busy right
now.'

The phone shrilled, and she ignored that, too—
until the answering machine kicked in and a gravelly voice said, 'Mrs Duncan, you really need to
answer your phone. We wouldn't want another
accident, would we?'

She went cold.

Michael's associates. Nobody else would call
her Mrs Duncan. But how had they got hold of
her number? She'd moved from the place she'd

shared with Michael, and her new number was ex-directory.

'As a children's nurse, you know how easily bones break.'

She had to suppress a whimper. That was a definite threat. They were going to hurt the children if she didn't do what they wanted.

'Mummy? Mummy, what's the matter?' Lexi asked.

'Nothing,' Rosie lied. 'I left the radio on in my bedroom.' She turned off the taps. 'Go and play in your bedroom for five minutes while I sort it out.'

She grabbed the phone and headed downstairs so the children wouldn't hear her. 'What do you want?' she whispered fiercely.

'About time you answered us, Mrs Duncan,' the gravelly voiced man said. 'You know what we want. What Michael owed us.'

'Michael's dead, and I don't have any money.'

'But your new boyfriend does. The Duke of Calvanera.'

'He's not my boyfriend,' Rosie said desperately.

'The papers are all saying he is.'

'The papers are just trying to sell copies. He isn't my boyfriend.'

'No? I believe the Duchess of Calvanera is quite frail. Imagine a fall and a broken hip at that age,' the man continued.

They were threatening Leo's mum as well as the children?

Fear made her feel queasy. But then she remembered her promise to herself after Michael's death: that nobody would ever make her feel a second-class citizen again. These people weren't going to bully her, either. 'I'm calling the police,' Rosie said.

There was a laugh from the other end of the line. 'You think they'll be able to do anything?'

'You threatened me. I'm recording every single word you say on my mobile phone,' Rosie lied.

'A recording proves nothing. But we know where you are. I'd advise you to talk to your boyfriend and get him to pay Michael's debts.'

The line went dead.

Oh, dear God. The nightmare that she'd thought was over had come back again. Except this time they'd been more explicit. They wanted money, or they'd hurt the children and Leo's mum.

She couldn't take that risk—but she also couldn't ask Leo to pay Michael's debts. And supposing the thugs decided they wanted interest as well? The only way she could think of to keep everyone safe was to end her relationship with Leo—and talk to the police. And even that might not be enough.

Florence had been perfect. Too perfect, maybe, because it had shown her the life she wanted. The future that maybe she could have with Leo. But the price was too high: she couldn't risk the safety of her children, Leo or Leo's mother.

She went back upstairs and chivvied the twins into the bathroom. They chattered away about the *palazzo* and the suit of armour, and Lexi was still clearly convinced that Leo was really a prince. It took three bedtime stories to calm them down. But finally the children fell asleep, and Rosie went into her own room, shutting the curtains in case the paparazzi tried to get some kind of blurry shot of her through the window.

And now she needed to talk to Leo.

It was a call she didn't want to make—a call that would break her dreams and trample her heart—but she couldn't see any other solution.

Leo answered straight away. 'Are you OK?'

No. Far from it. 'Yes.' She took a deep breath. 'Leo—we can't do this any more.' And these were the hardest words she was ever going to have to say. They actually stuck in her throat to the point where she thought she was going to choke, but finally she managed to compose herself. 'We have to end it.' Which would wipe out the threat to the children and his mother, and by extension to Leo himself. But she also knew she needed to give him an excuse that he'd accept instead of trying to solve. 'The press are going to make life too difficult. So I'd rather you didn't see me or the twins any more.'

'Rosie, this will blow over and people will have forgotten about it by the middle of the week. It's probably a slow news day.'

That was true. But she had to convince him. Tell him she didn't want the kind of life he could offer her—even though she did. 'There are photographers camped outside my house.'

'They'll get bored and go away.'

That was true, too. Digging her nails into her palm and reminding herself that she had to do this for everyone's safety, she demanded, 'When?

I can't camp out here until the middle of the week. I'm due at work tomorrow and the children are due at nursery school. I can't just ring in and say we're not turning up.'

'I'll send a car and get someone to escort you in.'

'No.' Because it wasn't really the press that was the problem. Maybe he'd understand if she dropped a hint about what really worried her. 'What if Michael's associates see the papers and crawl out of the woodwork?'

'They won't,' he reassured her. 'If they do try anything, I'll have the police onto them straight away—both in here and in Italy.'

Oh, but they had already. And the police wouldn't be able to help, Rosie was sure. Michael's associates were right in that she had no proof. 'You have a security team in Italy,' she said tentatively. 'Maybe you'd better make sure they take extra care with your mother.'

'Why?' His voice sharpened. 'Rosie, are you trying to tell me they've been in touch with you?'

Oh, help. She'd forgotten how quick his mind was. Of course he'd work it out for himself that she wasn't just being overprotective—that something had happened to worry her. 'No,' she lied. 'I just think you should take extra precautions— with yourself as well as with your mother. And you need to get your PR people to make a statement to the press, saying that we're nothing more to each other than colleagues.' Even though Leo could've been the centre of her life. She had to give him up. To keep him safe.

'But, Rosie—'

'No,' she cut in. Why did he have to make this so hard? Why couldn't he just walk away, the way he normally walked away from his girlfriends? 'I've thought about it and thought about it, and this is the only way. It has to end.' It was the last thing she wanted. But there was no other way. 'It has to end *now*. I'm sorry. Goodbye, Leo.'

She switched off her mobile phone after she cut the connection, and she ignored her landline when it shrilled.

How stupid she'd been, thinking she could escape Michael's shadow. It would always be there, and would always darken anything she did. And it wasn't fair to Leo or his family to expect them to deal with it, too.

The only way out of this was to end it between them.

Even though her heart felt as if someone had ripped it into tiny shreds and stomped on it and ground it into the floor. Because she'd fallen in love with Leo. Not the Duke—yes, the glitziness of the ball had been fun, but it wasn't who Leo was. She'd fallen for the man. The man who'd been so good with the twins. The man with the huge, huge heart. The man who really cared and wanted to make a difference to the world.

She wanted to be with him. But there just wasn't a way she could do that and keep everyone safe, and it wasn't fair to make everyone spend the rest of their days looking over their shoulders, worrying that her past was going to catch up with them. All that worry and mistrust would eat into their love like woodworm, little tiny bites at a time, and eventually what they felt for each other would simply crumble and fall apart, undermined by all the worry.

So she'd tell the children that Leo had had to go back to Italy, and she'd distract them every time they asked if they could go back to the *palazzo* to see him. And she'd hope that Leo could find the happiness he deserved with someone else— someone whose past wouldn't be a problem.

And even though she wanted to sob her heart out for what she'd lost, she didn't. Because some things hurt too much to cry.

Her last call was to the police. They sent someone to interview her, but it turned out that her fears were spot on: she didn't have anywhere near enough information to identify Michael's associates.

'We can check your phone records,' the policeman said, 'but we still might not be able to trace them. They might have used an unregistered mobile to call you.'

'Unregistered?' Rosie queried.

'Pay-as-you-go, bought with cash and with no ID to link to the phone. But if they do call you again, ring us straight away.'

'I will,' Rosie said, though it just made her feel hopeless.

And, when she went to bed that night, she couldn't sleep. She was haunted by that gravelly voice and the threat to her children and Leo's mother—three people who were too vulnerable to protect themselves. Then there was Leo himself. He was strong: but Michael's associates were capable of anything. She couldn't bear to think that they'd arrange an accident for him, the way she was sure they had for Michael. And how could you fight a nameless opponent, someone who stayed so deeply hidden in the shadows?

Hopefully Leo's PR team would get the word out that they weren't an item. Then Michael's associates would realise that he wasn't going to pay them, and they'd give up—just as they had when Michael had died.

And, although it broke her heart to do it, the alternative was worse. At least this way, Leo had the chance of finding happiness in the future. This way, Leo would be safe.

CHAPTER ELEVEN

THE PAPARAZZI WERE still outside Rosie's house the next morning, albeit not quite so many of them as there had been the previous evening. Rosie was much less worried about them than about the possible repercussions from Michael's former associates, but she took a taxi to the hospital instead of using the Tube, and she had a quiet word with the head of the nursery school about the situation and to ask for an extra layer of security for the twins.

And then it was time to face the ward.

'I saw you in the news this morning,' Kathleen said cheerfully. 'Loved the dress. So when did you and Leo get together?'

'We're not together,' Rosie said firmly. 'You know what the press is like. They add two and two and make a hundred.'

'But you went to Italy with him.'

'Yes,' Rosie admitted.

'Florence is really romantic.'

'I was looking at the Italian healthcare system and what we could learn from it,' Rosie fibbed. 'We went to a ball, yes, because it was to raise funds for a paediatric clinic that the Duke of Calvanera supports.'

Given that she so rarely went out on hospital evenings out, she really hoped that Kathleen would accept the story. Especially as most of it was true. To Rosie's relief, the other nurse simply smiled. 'Well, it was still a lovely dress.'

'Thank you,' Rosie said.

'So did you really save someone's life?'

Rosie grimaced. 'It wasn't just me. I was part of a team. And you would've done the same if someone had collapsed in front of you, wheezing and having trouble breathing, with a massive swelling on his hand where a wasp had stung him.'

'So you did save someone's life,' Kathleen said. 'Because that sounds like the beginning of anaphylaxis to me.'

'It was. Luckily he's fine now. And I'd better get my skates on.'

'You're on the allergy clinic this morning,' Kathleen said. 'With Leo.'

Rosie's heart sank. She'd known that she'd have to face Leo this week and they'd have to work together at some point, but she'd hoped for a little more time to prepare herself. To remind herself that no matter how attractive she found him, she had to put the safety of her children and his mother first.

'Nurse Hobbes,' Leo said, and gave her a cool little nod, when she rapped on the door and walked into the consulting room.

Formal was good. She could cope with that. 'Dr Marchetti.' Though she couldn't look him in the eye. Or the face, for that matter—because then she'd remember how his mouth had felt against her skin, and it would undermine her attempts to stay cool and calm in front of him. She looked down at the notes in her hand. 'I believe our first patient is Madison Turner, for the next session in her anti-venom treatment.'

How ironic. An allergy to wasps: just what had drawn the press's attention to her at the ball.

If Alessandro hadn't been stung, would she and Leo have got away with it? Or would the press still have tried to make up a story about them and Michael's associates would've crawled out of the woodwork anyway?

'If you'd like to bring Madison through, please,' Leo said, his voice cool.

When she sneaked a glance at him, Rosie realised that he was trying just as hard not to look at her. Guilt flooded through her as she realised she'd hurt him. But she hadn't dumped him because she didn't like him. Quite the opposite. She'd ended things with him solely to keep him, his family and the twins *safe*.

Not that she intended to discuss it with him. Talking about it wouldn't make things better—if he knew the full story, it might lead him to do something brave and reckless, and her sacrifice would've been for nothing. She couldn't bear to think of him being badly hurt. Or worse.

'I'll just go and get Madison,' she said.

She really hoped the tension between them didn't show, for the sake of their young patients and their parents. She did her best to be her usual professional self, and concentrated hard on getting the observations right and recording everything thoroughly. Leo barely spoke to her, except when he wanted some information from notes that she was using.

The rest of the morning's clinic was just as awkward. Rosie was glad to escape at lunchtime, and even more relieved that she had a cast-iron excuse to avoid Leo, because Monday was one of her days for reading to Penny.

'I saw your picture in the paper,' Julia said.

'It was a lot of fuss about nothing,' Rosie said with a smile. 'Any nurse would've done the same, in my shoes.'

'I didn't mean about the poor man who was stung. You were at that fancy ball with Leo Marchetti, weren't you?'

'As a colleague,' Rosie fibbed. In a desperate bid to divert Julia from the subject, she said, 'The sun's shining for once—you really should make the most of it. And I'm dying to find out what happens next in that ballet story, Penny.'

'Me, too!' the little girl said with a smile.

Thankfully Leo wasn't in the staff canteen when Rosie grabbed a sandwich and a cold drink from the kiosk before going back to the ward. But the afternoon allergy clinic was just as awkward as the morning's. She simply didn't know how to behave towards him. Friendly felt wrong, given that she'd just ended their relationship; but coolness felt wrong, too, as if she were adding insult to injury.

She was really glad when clinic ended and she was able to go down to the nursery school to pick up the twins.

'Was everything all right today?' she asked Nina, trying to damp down the anxiety in her voice. 'Nobody tried to…' *Take the twins.* She could barely get the words out.

'No. Everything was fine,' Nina reassured her. 'Is the press still hounding you?'

'I didn't go outside at lunchtime; it's my day to read to Penny,' Rosie said. Though even if it hadn't been, she wouldn't have gone outside. She planned to use a taxi to and from the hospital for the foreseeable future rather than taking the Tube, too, even though it was going to make a hole in her budget. The most important thing was that the children would be safe.

'I'm sure Leo can do something. Maybe his press team—'

'It'll be fine,' Rosie said with a smile. 'I'd better get the twins home. Thanks for everything, Nina.'

* * *

Leo was thoroughly miserable.

He missed Rosie.

And he missed the twins.

The weekend in Tuscany had been wonderful. Hearing children's laughter flood through the *palazzo*, watching the twins run around the gardens, seeing their delight in being allowed to touch the tiny suit of armour…

He'd actually felt like a father.

And, for the first time in his life, he'd actually wanted to be a father. Wanted to share his ancestral home with the next generation down. He'd loved showing Lexi and Freddie around.

Even more, he'd loved being with Rosie. Her quiet calmness. Her sweetness. The way she'd been unflappable at the ball, ignoring the fact that she was wearing haute couture and real diamonds and focusing instead on saving someone's life.

The sweetest bit for him had been dancing with her on the grass in the moonlight, just the two of them and the roses. And then making love with her. Losing himself in her. Falling asleep with her curled in his arms.

Yet ironically his home country had been the cause of their problems. If he hadn't taken Rosie to the ball, she wouldn't have caught the attention of the press.

She'd been pretty clear that it was over between them. That it had to be over, for the sake of her children. Although she'd put the blame on the press, she was obviously terrified that Michael's associates were going to crawl out of the woodwork and threaten the twins. And, for the second time in his life, Leo felt utterly powerless. The first time had been when his father had driven Emilia away, and Leo hadn't been able to convince her that he could keep her safe—that their love would be enough.

How ironic that he was in exactly the same position now. Except his family wasn't the problem: his mother had welcomed Rosie and the twins warmly, and he was pretty sure that Rosie had liked his mother, too. The problem was that Rosie was scared, and she couldn't get past the fear for long enough to let him solve the problem. Leo was pretty sure he could sort it out: a good lawyer would be able to get her an injunction. Even if she didn't know who they were, he'd be able to find out. Or his security team would.

This was crazy. He was supposed to be a doctor, a man who fixed things. Right now, he didn't have a clue how to fix this. How to make Rosie see that he *could* keep her safe. That everything would be just fine, if she'd give them a chance.

He'd just have to think harder. Work out what would be the one thing to make her trust him. But in the meantime he did what she'd asked and instructed his PR team to make it very clear that he and Rosie were absolutely not an item. And he had a quiet word with his legal and security team to see what they could find out about Michael and his associates, and to keep an eye on Rosie and the children. If the thugs really were watching her, his team would know very quickly—and he'd be able to keep Rosie and the children protected. And then maybe, once she realised that he could keep her safe, she'd learn to trust him.

Tuesday was just as difficult, Rosie found. Ward rounds, when she was rostered on with Leo; a staff meeting that spilled over into lunch and they all agreed to order in some sandwiches, so Rosie had to spend her lunch hour with Leo whether she liked it or not. She knew she had to speak to him, otherwise someone would notice the tension between them and start asking questions she didn't want to answer; but oh, it was hard. How did you make small talk with someone when you'd shared such a deep intimacy with them and remembered the feel of their skin against yours?

The worst thing was, she missed Leo. Like crazy. The children asked after him, too, wanting to know if he was coming to the park or if they were having pizza with him. Rosie was rapidly running out of excuses. And every lie ripped another little hole in her heart. If only she could be with him. If only she'd never met Michael— or if only Michael hadn't mixed with the wrong people because of his gambling problem…

But Wednesday morning brought her a different set of worries. The paparazzi and her fears about Michael's associates were forgotten when she went to wake up the twins and Freddie refused to get up.

Her son was often quiet, but he wasn't the grizzly sort.

'My tummy hurts,' he said.

And his face and hair were damp, she noticed. She sat down on the bed next to him and gently placed the back of her hand against his forehead.

It was definitely too hot.

'Does anywhere else hurt, Freddie?'

'Here.'

He pointed to his neck, and she went cold.

Had he just lain awkwardly during the night—or was it something more serious?

The first thing she needed to deal with was that temperature. And then she'd better call work to say that she couldn't come in, and the nursery school to say that the twins wouldn't be in today.

She grabbed the in-ear thermometer from the bathroom cabinet, along with the bottle of infant paracetamol. A quick check told her that her instincts were right: Freddie had a fever. 'I've got some special medicine to help you feel better,' she told Freddie, and measured out the dose. 'And I think you need to stay in bed this morning. If you're feeling a little bit better this afternoon, we'll all cuddle up on the sofa with a blanket and we'll watch *Toy Story*.' It was Freddie's favourite, guaranteed to cheer him up.

'I'm hot, Mummy,' he said.

'I know, baby.' She kissed his forehead. 'I'm going to get Lexi dressed, and then I'm going to bring you some juice.' It would be gentler on his stomach than milk. 'Do you want some toast? Or some yoghurt?'

He sniffed. 'No.'

'All right. I'll be back in a minute. Love you.'

'Love you, Mummy.' His lower lip wobbled, and a tear trickled down his cheek.

Once she'd got Lexi dressed, Rosie made her daughter some breakfast and grabbed the phone. Work was able to get agency cover for her, and the nursery school confirmed that a couple of children had gone down with some sort of tummy bug. Probably tomorrow both of them would be down with it, she thought wryly.

She'd just gone up to Freddie when he suddenly stiffened, twitched, and his eyes began to roll.

Oh, no.

'Freddie? Freddie?'

He didn't respond, and then the seizure began in earnest.

Pretend he's not yours. Pretend he's a patient, she reminded herself, and let her nursing training kick in. She glanced at her watch as she put him in the recovery position. OK. This was the first time he'd ever had a seizure—and he had a high temperature. Given his age, this was a perfectly normal thing.

As long as it lasted for less than five minutes.

She kept half an eye on him and half an eye on her watch. When the timing of the seizure reached seven minutes, she knew he needed better medical attention than she could give him at home. Given the time of day, it would be quicker for her to drive him to Paddington Children's Hospital herself rather than call an ambulance.

'Lexi, Freddie's not very well and we're going to take him in the car,' she said.

Somehow she managed to get both twins out to the car.

There were a couple of paparazzi loitering outside. 'Rosie!' one of them called. 'What's wrong?'

'My little boy's ill,' she said, pushing past them. 'Can't you find something better to do with your time than hassle me? I need to get him to hospital. Now!'

'Can we help?' the other one asked.

'Just go away. *Please*,' she said. She strapped the children into their car seats and hooked her phone up to her car's stereo system so she could make her phone calls safely. As soon as they were on the way to the hospital, she called the ward. 'Kathleen? It's Rosie. I'm bringing Freddie in with a febrile seizure.'

'Right. We'll be ready,' Kathleen said. 'Take care and we'll see you in a few minutes.'

'Thanks.' She cut the call and called her mother; to her relief, her mother answered on the fourth ring, and agreed to meet her at the hospital and take Lexi back home with her.

Just please, please let Freddie be all right, she thought grimly, and headed for the hospital.

'Was that Rosie?' Leo asked.

'Yes,' Kathleen confirmed.

'And she said that Freddie's ill?'

'Febrile convulsions.'

'I'll take the case,' he said.

'But—'

'I'm a doctor,' he said softly. 'And that comes before anything else. I'll look after Freddie.'

Though when Rosie appeared in the department, a couple of minutes later, carrying Freddie and with Lexi trotting along beside her, she didn't look particularly pleased to see him.

'I'm on duty. Treating children is my job,' he reminded her, taking Freddie from her and carrying the little boy over to one of the side rooms.

'Will you make Freddie better, Leo?' Lexi asked as he laid the little boy on the bed.

'I'll try my best,' he promised. Obviously Rosie hadn't had anyone who could look after her daughter at extremely short notice; at the same time, he needed to distract the little girl so he could find out exactly what symptoms Freddie had. 'Lexi, can you draw a picture of a dog for Freddie while I talk to your mummy, please?'

She nodded solemnly, and he gave her some paper and a pen.

'My mum's going to pick her up from here. She's on the way,' Rosie said.

'Not a problem,' Leo said gently. 'Kathleen said Freddie's had febrile convulsions. Can you give me a full history?'

'I'm probably overreacting,' she said, but he could hear the underlying panic in her voice. 'Freddie had a high temperature this morning, and he said his tummy and his neck hurt.'

A sore neck and a high temperature: that combination could mean something seriously nasty.

Clearly she was thinking the same thing, because she said, 'I checked and there's no rash.'

Though they both knew it was possible to have meningitis without a rash.

'I've given him a normal dose of infant paracetamol,' she said. 'It hasn't brought his temperature down. And then he started fitting.' She swallowed hard. 'Neither of the twins has ever had any kind of fit before. I know he's of the age when he's most likely to have a febrile seizure, but it went on for more than ten minutes.'

'And you did exactly the right thing bringing him in. You're a paediatric nurse, so you know it's really common and most of the time everything's fine.'

But he could see in her expression that she was thinking of the rare cases when everything wasn't fine.

'It could be a bacterial infection causing the temperature and the fit,' he said. 'Not necessarily meningitis: it could be a urinary tract infection, an upper respiratory tract infection or tonsillitis, an ear infection or gastroenteritis.'

She dragged in a breath. 'But it could be meningitis—you know a rash isn't the only sign.'

He nodded. 'Did Freddie have a vaccination for meningitis C?'

'Yes, at twelve weeks and again at a year,' Rosie confirmed.

'Again, that's a good sign,' he said gently. Small children didn't always get the classic triad of meningitis, but it was worth asking. 'Apart from saying his neck's sore, has he shown any signs of confusion, or a dislike of bright lights?' When Rosie shook her head he continued, 'Has he had any pains in his legs? Are his hands and feet cold, or has he said they feel cold?'

'No.'

'Again, that's a really good sign.' He checked Freddie's temperature, heart rate and capillary refill, and looked in his ears. 'Did he show any signs of pallor before the fit, or has there been any change in the colour of his lips?'

'No.'

'That's good.' But Leo also noted that Freddie wasn't smiling, and he was very quiet. Was that because the little boy had gone back into his shell or simply because he wasn't feeling well?

'I'm going to take a urine sample for culture,' he said. 'Given what you've told me, I'm not going to take any risks and I'll treat him for suspected meningitis until I can find out what the problem is. I'll need to do a lumbar puncture.'

Rosie went white.

How Leo wanted to hold her. Tightly.

But right now it wasn't appropriate. He needed to be a doctor first. 'You know the drill,' he said, 'and you also know it takes a couple of days to get the test results back, so I'll need to admit him to the ward. I'll start him on antibiotics and I might put him on a drip if I'm not happy with his hydration. I'll give him antipyretics as well, so I need you to tell me exactly when you gave the last dose, and I'll need you to sign the consent form.'

'All right,' Rosie said.

There was a knock on the door and an older woman stood in the doorway. 'Rosie?'

'Thanks for coming, Mum.'

Even if Rosie hadn't spoken, Leo would've known exactly who the older woman was; she had the same bright blue eyes as Rosie and her hair would've been the same colour years ago.

Rosie was clearly trying her best to keep it together in front of the twins, but Leo could see the strain in her eyes.

'Mrs Hobbes. I'm Dr Marchetti—Leo,' he said.

He could see the moment that the penny dropped. Yes, he was *that* Leo. 'Take care of our Freddie,' Mrs Hobbes said quietly.

'I will,' he promised.

'Lexi, are you ready to go with Nanna?' Rosie asked.

The little girl nodded. 'Freddie, I drawed you a doggie to make you better.' She handed the picture to her twin and gave the pen back to Leo.

'Mum—before you go.' Rosie lowered her voice, as did Mrs Hobbes, but Leo caught every word they said. 'Just be careful. Michael—those men...'

Mrs Hobbes looked grim. 'Have you told the police?'

'They said to call them if I got another call. But just... Be careful, Mum.'

'She'll be safe with me,' Mrs Hobbes promised. She turned to Lexi. 'Come on, sweetie. We'll go back to my house now, and Mummy can text us to let us know how Freddie is.'

Lexi took her hand and left the room beside her grandmother.

Leo really wanted to talk to Rosie about Michael's associates, but it would have to wait; he needed to treat Freddie first. But then he'd deal with the situation. Because now he knew exactly why Rosie had ended things between them—and he had a pretty good idea why she hadn't told him the full story.

'Freddie, I'm going to take a little bit of fluid from your back so I can do some tests,' Leo said. 'I've got some special cream, so it won't hurt.'

'Promise?' Freddie asked.

'Promise,' Leo said solemnly.

'Will you sing me a song?'

If it would distract the boy, it was a great idea. 'Sure I will, while Mummy holds your hand,' he said, and sang Freddie all the nursery songs he knew in Italian and English while he performed the lumbar puncture.

'All done,' he said, and then he saw that Rosie was crying. Silently, but the tears were running down her face.

Ah, hell.

He couldn't just ignore it.

He wrapped his arms round her.

She pulled away. 'This isn't appropriate.'

'Yes, it is,' he said softly. 'You're my colleague, you're on your own and you're upset. I'm not an unfeeling monster who can walk away from that, regardless of whatever else might have happened.'

She leaned her head against his shoulder for just a moment, as if wishing that she really could rely on him, then pulled away. 'I have to be strong, for Freddie's sake.'

'But you don't have to be alone,' he reminded her. 'I'm here. Any time you need me.' And he wanted her and the twins in his life. For good.

He wasn't going to put pressure on her now, but once Freddie was on the mend they could discuss it. In the meantime he would just be there for her. No strings, no talking. Just there.

'Rosie—I heard what you said to your mum.'

She looked away. 'It's not your problem.'

'I can help. Right now you've got more than enough on your plate. Let me take some of the burden.'

'I can't.'

He sighed. 'There aren't any strings, if that's

what you're worried about. Look, it's my fault that they've been in touch with you. If you hadn't come to Italy with me, the press wouldn't have heard about you, and Michael's associates wouldn't have contacted you. So, actually, it *is* my problem.'

She looked utterly miserable. 'I need to concentrate on Freddie.'

'Exactly. Let me deal with this so you can concentrate on him instead of worrying.'

She looked torn, but finally she said, 'All right. And thank you.'

He hated the way she sounded so broken and defeated. But, once Freddie was on the mend, she'd have that layer of worry removed. In the meantime he'd do his best to support her. And he'd solve her problem with Michael's associates.

The following two days were the worst forty-eight hours of Rosie's life. It was hard to keep Freddie's temperature down, and even though he was on antibiotics she worried that it really might be meningitis. If she lost him...

Leo kept a close eye on Freddie, and he also brought in sandwiches and coffee for Rosie.

'I can't eat,' she said.

'You have to, if you want to be strong for Freddie.'

But she couldn't face eating anything, not when she was so worried. And she didn't want to leave her little boy that night, so Leo made sure she had blankets and fresh water.

'I'll stay with you,' he said.

And how tempting it was. The idea of being able to lean on him, having someone there to support her. But she'd ended it between them. She couldn't be that selfish. 'No. You're on duty. You need a proper sleep.'

'I've done my time as a junior doctor. I can sleep in a chair.'

How she wanted to say yes. 'Thank you, but we'll be fine.'

'OK. Call me if you need me.'

At three in the morning, she thought about what he'd said. She was bone-deep tired, but how could she possibly sleep when her little boy was so sick? And it wouldn't be fair to call Leo, just because she felt alone and helpless. He'd offered, and she knew he'd be there within minutes if she called him. But it just wouldn't be fair of her.

Her eyes felt gritty from lack of sleep the next morning. And then Leo walked in with a paper cup of coffee from Tony's, fresh pastries and a pot of prepared strawberries, raspberries and blueberries.

She stared at him, unable to pull any coherent words together.

'Eat,' he said. 'I'm pulling rank as your senior colleague. You need to eat.' He glanced down at the sleeping child. 'I'm not leaving until you've eaten at least half the food and drunk that coffee.'

She knew he meant it. And although he didn't make her talk to him—he spent his time looking through Freddie's chart—having him there did make her feel better. Less alone.

'Better?' he asked when she'd managed to force down the fruit and one of the pastries.

'Better.'

'Good. Go and have a shower.' He produced a toothbrush and toothpaste. 'Hospital shop, before you ask. It'll make you feel a bit more human. I won't be going anywhere until you're back.'

'If he wakes—'

'—then I'll tell him where you are. Stop worrying.'

Gratefully, she took a shower and cleaned her teeth. Although she didn't have fresh clothes, just the shower and cleaning her teeth made her feel better. And the fact that Leo cared enough to do that for her, even though she'd dumped him…

She scrubbed the tears away. Not now. She had to stay strong.

'Thank you,' she said when she got back to Freddie's bedside to discover that he was still asleep.

'Any time. Hopefully the antibiotics will start to make a difference today. I'll drop by later,' Leo said.

And he was as good as his word. He called in twice to see how Freddie was doing. He also made her go out for a walk at lunchtime while he sat with Freddie.

'But—'

'But nothing,' he cut in gently. 'This is what you do for Julia. Let me do the same for you.'

'What about the press?'

'What about them? I'm a doctor first and a duke second. I couldn't care less about what the press thinks. You, Freddie and Lexi are the important ones here,' he told her. 'And Freddie knows me. He knows I'll do my best for him.'

She couldn't fault Leo as a doctor. He'd been meticulous with all the children they'd treated together, and he'd kept a really close eye on Freddie.

'But, just so you know,' he added, 'I've spoken to my PR team. They're dealing with the press and you don't have to worry any more.'

Maybe not about the press. But medicine was another matter: small children could become very sick, very quickly. And there was still the issue of Michael's associates.

As if he guessed at the fear she'd left unspoken, he said, 'I've also spoken to my security team and my lawyers. They've talked to the police here and they've been doing some investigations of their own. We know who they are. There's an injunction in place now, and my security team is keeping an eye on you, so nobody can get anywhere near you, Lexi or Freddie. You're *safe.*'

She couldn't take it in. Any of it. Everything felt like a blur. He knew who they were? But how? How had his team managed to find out who Michael's associates were, when the police hadn't been able to help her?

'Right. Out,' he said, gesturing to the door. 'Go and get some fresh air.'

Rosie did as she was told, her feet practically on autopilot. She wandered aimlessly round the streets outside the hospital, but all she could think of was Freddie. Her little boy. Was he going to be all right?

Unable to bear being away from him any longer, she went back in to the ward, only to find Freddie holding Leo's hand and Leo telling him some story about castles and magic suits of armour.

'Mummy.' Freddie gave her a half-smile and relief washed through Rosie. Was he really getting better? Or was this a slight recovery before he got worse?

There was a knock on the door, and Julia leaned round the doorframe. 'Hi. I won't stop—but Penny heard that Nurse Rosie's little boy wasn't very well, so she's done a drawing for him.' She smiled. 'She wanted to come herself, but...'

'The risk of infection's too great. I understand,' Rosie said, and took the drawing. 'Please say thank you to her. Look, Freddie—Penny's done you a special drawing of a doggie.'

'I like doggies,' he said. 'Thank you.'

She had to hold back the tears.

Leo squeezed her shoulder and murmured, 'It's going to be all right, Rosie, I promise you.'

He brought in a selection of savouries from one of the local cafés to tempt her that evening; and again he made her go out for some fresh air when Freddie fell asleep.

'You haven't slept for a day and a half,' he said when she came back all of ten minutes later. 'Take a nap now.'

'But—'

'I'm here. I'm not going anywhere. Freddie's safe with me. Sleep,' he said.

'I...' She shook her head. 'I can't.'

'Then let's try it this way.' He scooped her up in his arms and sat down in the chair next to Freddie's bed, then settled her on his lap and held her close.

'Leo, we can't—'

'Yes, we can,' he said, completely implacable. 'Go to sleep.'

Rosie didn't think it was possible; but whether

it was the warmth of Leo's body, the regularity of his breathing or just the fact that she felt safe, curled in his arms like this, she actually fell asleep.

For four hours.

'I'm so sorry,' she said when she woke and realised how late it was.

'Don't apologise. You needed that.'

'But you should've gone home hours ago.'

'To an empty flat.' His eyes were very dark. 'I'm right where I want to be. By your side.'

'But we…' She swallowed hard. 'We're not together.'

'We could be,' he said.

She dragged in a breath. 'It's too complicated.'

'Then let me make it simple for you,' he said. 'I grew up in a world where I didn't know who I was supposed to be—my father changed the goalposts constantly, and nothing I did was ever right. I thought it was me, and that I was unlovable. Emilia made me think that maybe the problem wasn't me after all, and love might actually exist—but it was so easy for my father to push her out of my life. So I decided that a family wasn't for me. I didn't want to bring children into

the mean-spirited world I'd grown up in. And I
didn't want to make some kind of dynastic marriage with someone I didn't love and then start
making the same mistakes my father did.' He
stroked her face. 'And then I met you. And the
twins. And suddenly everything was possible.
Love and a family… Everything I'd told myself
I didn't want, but actually I did. And when you
came to Tuscany, it was the first time I could remember feeling really happy at the *palazzo*. Having the place full of the twins' laughter, sharing
the garden with you.' He looked her straight in
the eye. 'Making love with you and falling asleep
with you in my arms. It was perfect.'

It had been like that for her, too.

'And, at the charity ball, I was so proud of you.
You saved someone's life—you didn't fuss about
your dress or anything, you were just cool and
calm and sorted everything out, even though
you didn't speak the language. I love you, Rosie.
You're everything I want—you and the twins.
We can give them a fabulous life together—and
you're the one who can help me make the world
a better place. Marry me, Rosie.'

Words she'd never thought to hear again.

And she knew Leo wouldn't change. He'd be there right by her side. He'd stick to his vows to love, honour and cherish her.

How she wanted to say yes.

But there was her past. Michael. The press had dredged it up once, and they'd do it again and again. She'd end up dragging Leo down. She remembered him saying that he'd fixed the problem with Michael's associates—but supposing it was only temporary? Supposing they came back? Supposing they regrouped and wanted more and more? Supposing they got past Leo's security and hurt the children, his mother or him?

'I can't,' she whispered.

She tried to wriggle off his lap, but he wouldn't let her. 'Why not?'

Did he really need her to spell it out? 'I can't fit into your world. I'd drag you down.'

He kissed her. 'No, you wouldn't. You've changed my world, Rosie. You've shown me what love and family really means. My mother adores you—so does everyone at the *palazzo*.'

Could it possibly be true? She'd really made a difference to his world? He really, really wanted her there?

'Through you, I've realised that I can give our children a life like the one I didn't have when I was growing up—one where their parents love and respect each other. One where we'll be firm when we have to, but fair, and our children will always know we love them and want to have fun with them.' He paused. 'I love you, Rosie.'

He loved her.

She could see the sincerity in his dark eyes. He felt the same way about her that she did about him. Something that went deeper than the fear that numbed her every time she thought about what Michael's associates could do.

Didn't they say that love could conquer all?

Looking at Leo, she saw strength and compassion and deep, deep love.

And that gave her the courage to admit to her feelings. 'I love you, too, Leo,' she whispered. He was everything she wanted—a man who'd be there in the tough times as well as the good times, reliable and kind and having time for the children. A man who really loved her instead of just expecting her to be some kind of trophy wife.

'Then marry me, Rosie. Forget the dukedom.

It's not important. At the end of the day, I'm a doctor and you're a nurse. We're a team at work and we'll be a great team at home, too. And I don't care whether we live in London or Italy: as long as I'm with you, I'll be happy. And I can make you and the twins happy, too. Keep you safe. Make you feel loved and respected, the way you deserve to be.'

Even though she was sleep-deprived and had spent the last couple of days worried sick, she was mentally together just enough to realise that he meant it.

They really could have it all.

Be a real family.

But there was still that one last fear. The one thing that stopped her being able to step forward and take what he was offering her. 'Michael's associates... How could you fix it, when the police couldn't? How could you find out who they were?'

He stroked her face. 'I don't like the man my father was, but maybe he's done us a good turn, in the end.'

'How?' She didn't understand.

'His reputation apparently still has a ripple or

two,' Leo said dryly. 'His name is definitely re-membered in certain circles. And let's just say that my team have, um, avenues open to them that might not be available elsewhere. So I be-lieve them when they tell me that nobody will ever threaten you or the children, ever again. You're safe with me. Always. Marry me, Rosie.'

You're safe with me.

She believed him. 'Yes,' she whispered.

He stroked her face. 'You're sure?'

'I'm sure.' She dragged in a breath. 'I'll be honest—I'm still scared that somehow Michael's associates will find a way round your security team. That they'll hurt you. But if you're pre-pared to take that risk, then I can be brave, too.'

'The alternative's being without you. Missing you every single second of every single day. And I don't want to do that,' he said simply. 'And they won't find a way round my security team. As I said, my father was, um, good at warning people off. I'm not my father, but people will remem-ber him. And maybe we can turn his legacy into love. Together.'

'Together,' she echoed, and reached up to kiss him.

* * *

Leo stayed with Rosie that night, curled together in a chair.

And in the morning, they got the news they'd both been hoping for.

'It isn't meningitis,' Leo said, and lifted her up and whirled her round. 'We're still not sure what the virus is, but provided his temperature stays down and he keeps responding the way he has, you can take him home at lunchtime.'

'The perfect day,' she said. 'Freddie's all right. And we have a wedding to plan.'

He kissed her lingeringly. 'The perfect day.'

EPILOGUE

One year later

'YOU'RE QUITE SURE you don't mind looking after the children tonight?' Rosie asked her mother-in-law.

'Very sure. You know I love spending time with my grandchildren,' Beatrice said.

'And we like being with Nonna,' Freddie and Lexi added.

Since they'd moved to Florence, where Leo had taken over as the head of the clinic that the Marchetti family supported and Rosie worked there as a nurse, the children had really blossomed. They were almost as fluent in Italian as they were in English. And Rosie rather thought that Beatrice had blossomed, too; she seemed much less frail. Confident enough to come and stay in Leo and Rosie's townhouse in Florence for the night, while they attended the clinic's annual charity ball. And, best of all, her past was staying exactly where she wanted it to stay: in the past. True to Leo's promise, Michael's associates had left her alone.

'Now, off to the ball with you,' Beatrice said. 'And hopefully there will be no wasps, tonight.'

'Hopefully,' Leo said with a smile. 'Though Rosie can ask for adrenaline herself now in Italian, thanks to your teaching, Mamma.'

'Ah, now I leave the medical terminology to you, Leo,' Beatrice said with a smile. 'You look lovely in that dress, Rosie. I'm so proud of my new daughter.'

'And thank you for lending me your diamonds again, Mamma,' Rosie said, hugging her warmly.

'It's good to see them being worn. Just as they should be, by the Duchessa di Calvanera,' Beatrice said.

'Send us some pictures from the ball,' Lexi begged, 'so we can see all the other pretty dresses, too.'

'We'll try. Be good for Nonna,' Leo said.

'Sì, Babbo,' the twins chorused.

Rosie was still smiling when Leo drove them across town to the hotel. 'Funny to think it's a year since my first trip to Florence. And what a year it's been. Our wedding, moving here to work in the clinic…'

'It's been a good year,' Leo agreed, parking the car.

'Just before we go in,' she said, 'I have a little news for you.'

'Oh?'

'You might need to brush up on your nappy-changing skills.'

He stared at her. 'Nappy-changing?'

She spread her hands. 'This is the twenty-first century. Duke or not, I'm expecting you to be a fully hands-on dad.'

'Hands-on…?' The penny finally dropped, and he punched his fist in the air. 'We're going to have another baby!'

Which was when Rosie realised that Leo really *did* think of the twins as his own. He'd always been careful to treat them as if they were his own children; and now she knew he loved them as much as she did.

'You,' he said, 'have just made me happier than I ever thought possible. I know we're not supposed to breathe a word until twelve weeks, but right now I want to climb to the top of the hotel and yell out to the whole of Florence that I'm going to be a dad again. And that I love my wife very, very much. And...'

There was only one way to stop her over-talkative Duke.

She smiled, and kissed him.

* * * * *

Welcome to the
PADDINGTON CHILDREN'S HOSPITAL
six-book series

Available now:

THEIR ONE NIGHT BABY
by Carol Marinelli
FORBIDDEN TO THE PLAYBOY SURGEON
by Fiona Lowe
MUMMY, NURSE...DUCHESS?
by Kate Hardy
FALLING FOR THE FOSTER MUM
by Karin Baine

Coming soon:

HEALING THE SHEIKH'S HEART
by Annie O'Neil
A LIFE-SAVING REUNION
by Alison Roberts

MILLS & BOON®
Large Print Medical

December

Healing the Sheikh's Heart	Annie O'Neil
A Life-Saving Reunion	Alison Roberts
The Surgeon's Cinderella	Susan Carlisle
Saved by Doctor Dreamy	Dianne Drake
Pregnant with the Boss's Baby	Sue MacKay
Reunited with His Runaway Doc	Lucy Clark

January

The Surrogate's Unexpected Miracle	Alison Roberts
Convenient Marriage, Surprise Twins	Amy Ruttan
The Doctor's Secret Son	Janice Lynn
Reforming the Playboy	Karin Baine
Their Double Baby Gift	Louisa Heaton
Saving Baby Amy	Annie Claydon

February

Tempted by the Bridesmaid	Annie O'Neil
Claiming His Pregnant Princess	Annie O'Neil
A Miracle for the Baby Doctor	Meredith Webber
Stolen Kisses with Her Boss	Susan Carlisle
Encounter with a Commanding Officer	Charlotte Hawkes
Rebel Doc on Her Doorstep	Lucy Ryder

MILLS & BOON®
Large Print Medical

March

The Doctor's Forbidden Temptation	Tina Beckett
From Passion to Pregnancy	Tina Beckett
The Midwife's Longed-For Baby	Caroline Anderson
One Night That Changed Her Life	Emily Forbes
The Prince's Cinderella Bride	Amalie Berlin
Bride for the Single Dad	Jennifer Taylor

April

Sleigh Ride with the Single Dad	Alison Roberts
A Firefighter in Her Stocking	Janice Lynn
A Christmas Miracle	Amy Andrews
Reunited with Her Surgeon Prince	Marion Lennox
Falling for Her Fake Fiancé	Sue MacKay
The Family She's Longed For	Lucy Clark

May

The Spanish Duke's Holiday Proposal	Robin Gianna
The Rescue Doc's Christmas Miracle	Amalie Berlin
Christmas with Her Daredevil Doc	Kate Hardy
Their Pregnancy Gift	Kate Hardy
A Family Made at Christmas	Scarlet Wilson
Their Mistletoe Baby	Karin Baine

MILLS & BOON®
Large Print – November 2017

ROMANCE

An Heir Made in the Marriage Bed	Anne Mather
The Prince's Stolen Virgin	Maisey Yates
Protecting His Defiant Innocent	Michelle Smart
Pregnant at Acosta's Demand	Maya Blake
The Secret He Must Claim	Chantelle Shaw
Carrying the Spaniard's Child	Jennie Lucas
A Ring for the Greek's Baby	Melanie Milburne
The Runaway Bride and the Billionaire	Kate Hardy
The Boss's Fake Fiancée	Susan Meier
The Millionaire's Redemption	Therese Beharrie
Captivated by the Enigmatic Tycoon	Bella Bucannon

HISTORICAL

Marrying His Cinderella Countess	Louise Allen
A Ring for the Pregnant Debutante	Laura Martin
The Governess Heiress	Elizabeth Beacon
The Warrior's Damsel in Distress	Meriel Fuller
The Knight's Scarred Maiden	Nicole Locke

MEDICAL

Healing the Sheikh's Heart	Annie O'Neil
A Life-Saving Reunion	Alison Roberts
The Surgeon's Cinderella	Susan Carlisle
Saved by Doctor Dreamy	Dianne Drake
Pregnant with the Boss's Baby	Sue MacKay
Reunited with His Runaway Doc	Lucy Clark

MILLS & BOON®

Why shop at millsandboon.co.uk?

Each year, thousands of romance readers find their perfect read at millsandboon.co.uk. That's because we're passionate about bringing you the very best romantic fiction. Here are some of the advantages of shopping at www.millsandboon.co.uk:

* **Get new books first**—you'll be able to buy your favourite books one month before they hit the shops

* **Get exclusive discounts**—you'll also be able to buy our specially created monthly collections, with up to 50% off the RRP

* **Find your favourite authors**—latest news, interviews and new releases for all your favourite authors and series on our website, plus ideas for what to try next

* **Join in**—once you've bought your favourite books, don't forget to register with us to rate, review and join in the discussions

Visit **www.millsandboon.co.uk**
for all this and more today!